CLUB CSI:

The Case of the Digital Deception

by Ellie O'Ryan

Simon Spotlight

New York   London   Toronto   Sydney   New Delhi

SIMON SPOTLIGHT

An imprint of Simon & Schuster Children's Publishing Division
1230 Avenue of the Americas, New York, New York 10020
© 2013 by CBS Broadcasting Inc. and Entertainment AB Funding LLC.
All Rights Reserved. CSI: CRIME SCENE INVESTIGATION in USA is a
trademark of CBS Broadcasting Inc. and outside USA is a trademark of
Entertainment AB Funding LLC.
All rights reserved, including the right of reproduction in whole or
in part in any form. SIMON SPOTLIGHT and colophon are registered
trademarks of Simon & Schuster, Inc. For information about special
discounts for bulk purchases, please contact Simon & Schuster
Special Sales at 1-866-506-1949 or business@simonandschuster.com.
Manufactured in the United States of America 1212 OFF
First Edition 10 9 8 7 6 5 4 3 2 1
ISBN 978-1-4424-7257-0 (pbk)
ISBN 978-1-4424-7258-7 (hc)
ISBN 978-1-4424-7259-4 (eBook)
Library of Congress Control Number 2012938001

Chapter 1

It was an ordinary Tuesday morning at Woodlands Junior High and Corey had one thing on his mind: lunch. He couldn't help it. The smell of spices and warm food wafted through the hallways, making his stomach growl. Corey was so focused on lunch, he didn't even notice when his friends Ben and Hannah turned and walked into Miss Hodges's classroom and he kept going straight—toward the cafeteria!

"Uh, Corey?" Ben called to him from the doorway. "We still have another period until lunchtime."

Corey turned around and grinned sheepishly. He was so hungry that he almost forgot about his favorite class, forensic science with Miss Hodges. But he wasn't all that embarrassed. If anyone knew how much Corey loved lunch, it was Ben. Along with Hannah, he and Ben had been best friends since elementary school. And now they were something else, too—members of Club CSI.

It all started when a new science teacher, Miss Hodges, came to Woodlands. Her forensic science class was so fascinating that it had inspired Ben, Corey, and Hannah to start Club CSI. With Miss Hodges as their advisor, the best friends had decided to use what they learned in class to investigate the mysteries and crimes that sometimes happened at their school.

When Corey and Ben entered the classroom, Hannah was already sitting at her desk. "Glad you're joining us, Corey," she teased. "It's going to be a fun class. I think we're starting a new unit today."

"I can't wait," said Ben. "Any idea what it's about?"

Hannah shook her head. So far, Miss Hodges had taught her class about securing a crime scene, handwriting and shoeprint analysis, fingerprinting techniques, and many other tools of a crime-scene investigator, but Club CSI had already realized that the more they knew about forensic science, the more there was to learn.

Miss Hodges strode into the room just as the bell rang. All the students quieted down as she stood in the front of the class.

"Let's jump right in, shall we?" Miss Hodges began. "I've been getting a lot of questions about the process of interviewing suspects. So I thought we'd start a unit on behavioral science, which, for our purposes, can be defined as the study of human behavior through observation."

Miss Hodges paused so everyone could write down the definition.

"Behavioral science is extremely important for Crime Scene Investigators, especially when they're conducting interviews of suspects and witnesses," Miss Hodges said. "We'll spend today's class talking about what CSIs look for during an interview."

Under his desk, Corey did a secret fist-pump. During Club CSI's past investigations, he'd started taking the lead in interviews—and he loved it. Corey was so friendly and easygoing that people really opened up to him. He loved the challenge of asking just the right questions in just the right way. Corey hoped he'd become an even better investigator after learning about how CSIs interview people.

"You all know that one of the most essential elements of the job is interviewing potential suspects," Miss Hodges continued. "During these interviews, investigators can't just rely on the suspect's answers. They must also observe the suspect's behavior during the questioning. In other words, investigators are paying attention to *what* the suspect says—and *how* he or she says it."

Miss Hodges wrote "body language" on the board.

"Who can tell me what body language is?" Miss Hodges asked.

Hannah raised her hand first. "It's a way you can communicate without talking," she explained. "Like, if you cross your arms, your body language might make you look mean or unfriendly."

"Good," Miss Hodges said. "And there are some actions or mannerisms that are associated with lying. Now, I'm going to need two volunteers." A bunch of hands shot into the air. "Let's have . . . Ricky . . . and Charlie. Boys, let's step into the hallway."

A few moments later Miss Hodges returned, with Ricky and Charlie following her. "We're going to do a little experiment," she announced. "Ricky and

Charlie will be the suspects. One of them will tell the truth, and the other will answer every question with a lie. The rest of the class will be the investigators. You can ask Charlie and Ricky all about themselves. During the questioning, I want you to observe them very carefully—and then we'll talk about your observations."

Corey jumped right in. "What's your favorite color?"

"Green," Charlie replied.

"Uh, red," Ricky said.

"And what's your favorite food?" Ben asked.

"That's a tough one," Charlie said. "Tacos, I guess."

Ricky licked his lips. "Stew."

"What's your favorite sport?" asked Katie.

"Hockey," Charlie answered.

"Baseball. Definitely," Ricky said, after glancing out the window to where the gym class was playing a game.

One by one, each student in the class had a chance to ask the "suspects" a question. But Corey had more questions than anyone. His eyes never left Charlie and Ricky, not even when he scribbled notes.

"Okay, I think those are enough questions for now," Miss Hodges finally said. "Who would like to tell the class about their observations? Corey, you took a lot of notes."

Corey nodded vigorously. "I think Ricky was lying!" he said in a rush.

"Wait a minute. Are you calling me a *liar*?" Ricky shot back. "What proof do you have?"

Hannah noticed right away that Ricky's eyes were twinkling, like he was enjoying himself.

Corey didn't miss a beat. "Oh, I think I have proof," he said, staring at his notebook. "It's all . . . right . . . here. . . . Hang on a second. . . ."

The class waited expectantly while Corey peered at his notes. Finally, he looked up. "Sorry. I'm having a little trouble reading my own writing!" he said.

Everyone cracked up; even Miss Hodges smiled. "That's okay, Corey. Do you remember what Ricky said that made you think he was lying?" she asked.

"It wasn't really anything he said," Corey told her. "But—here it is—every time he answered, Ricky did something weird. Like, he glanced out the window four times, he said 'uh' or 'um' nine times, and he licked his lips fourteen times before he spoke. But

Charlie wasn't doing any of those things."

"Excellent observations, Corey!" Miss Hodges exclaimed. "Those are all physical signs that someone might be lying. For example, people often say 'um' to buy time to think up a lie, or they'll glance around looking for inspiration." She turned to Corey. "Were there any answers, however, in particular that made you think Ricky was lying?"

Corey's eyes darted back and forth as he scanned his notes. "Uh . . . I guess I was so busy writing down Ricky's and Charlie's body language that I didn't pay enough attention to their answers!" he admitted sheepishly.

As everyone laughed again, Ben raised his hand. "I noticed something," he said. "Charlie said his favorite color was green, right? And his backpack is green. So that made sense. Then Ricky said his favorite color is red . . . but his backpack, shoes, and hat are all blue. If red really was Ricky's favorite color, I think he'd have more red stuff."

Miss Hodges nodded. "That's a good point, Ben, and it shows us that the strongest conclusions are based on multiple types of observations. Now, none of this is hard evidence that Ricky was lying. Maybe all the red backpacks were sold out that day. Maybe Ricky was licking his lips because they're dry. But the way Corey and Ben put together their observations to establish a possible pattern of untruthfulness is what any investigator would do."

"So were you lying?" Ben asked Ricky.

Ricky stared at him for a long moment. Then a big smile broke across his face. "Yeah! I was the liar! Guilty as charged!" he bragged.

"Remember, just because someone lies during an interrogation doesn't mean that he or she is guilty of a crime," Miss Hodges spoke up quickly. "People lie during investigations for all sorts of reasons that have nothing to do with the crime. But lying during questioning will definitely influence an investigator to dig a little deeper."

. Miss Hodges returned to the board and started writing a list.

Fidgeting
Avoiding eye contact
Stalling or pausing before answering
   (saying "uh," "um," "er")
Stammering or stumbling over words

Covering one's mouth while speaking

Touching one's face, head, or mouth while speaking

Defensive responses

Repeating the question before answering or answering questions with questions

Tense or anxious behavior

Answers that are vague or seem rehearsed

"These are some common signs that someone might be lying," Miss Hodges explained as she placed a stack of handouts on her desk. "Often, they are subconscious—that means that the person who's lying isn't even aware that he or she is doing them. And it's important to remember that someone displaying these signs might really be telling the truth—or that someone might be lying without showing any observable signs."

Ben raised his hand.

"Yes, Ben?" Miss Hodges said.

"How do you *know*, then?" he asked. "If the signs aren't always reliable . . . how can you really *know* if someone is lying?"

"You can't," Miss Hodges answered him. "Life

would certainly be a lot easier for CSIs if you could!"

Miss Hodges waited for the class to finish chuckling before she continued. "Now, for homework tonight, I'd like you to read this article about deception and body language. The most important knowledge you can take away from this lesson is that CSIs must heighten their observation skills, especially during interviews," she explained as she placed a stack of handouts on her desk. "You never know when a suspect will accidentally reveal a lie that could be the key to solving a case."

After the bell rang, the students hurried off to the cafeteria with Corey leading the way. He weaved in and out of the crowds like a quarterback rushing to the end zone. By the time Hannah and Ben sat down with their food, Corey was already halfway through his chickpea curry.

Hannah looked a little sick as she watched Corey shovel food into his mouth. Finally, she said, "Um, Corey? You want to slow down a little, maybe?"

"Sorry," Corey said through a big bite of food, accidentally spraying a few chewed-up chickpeas across the table. Corey swallowed hard. "Oops. Double sorry."

Hannah rolled her eyes jokingly, and Ben started to laugh as he passed a napkin to his friend. "Why the rush?" Ben asked.

"Seconds," Corey explained. He pointed at the dwindling lunch line. "I have to finish eating my first serving by twelve-seventeen so that I can be back in line by twelve-twenty for seconds. If you get there past twelve twenty-five, forget it. There won't be anything left."

"Sounds like you have it all figured out," Hannah replied. "But I still don't get the rush. The timing never mattered before, did it?"

Corey shook his head. "Not before the menu changed," he said. Then he took one more giant bite and grabbed his tray. "Back in a sec."

As Corey strode through the cafeteria, he thought of all the new dishes Mrs. Collins, the cafeteria chef, had served lately. Pad thai . . . margherita pizza . . . grilled corn on the cob . . . It was hard to pick a favorite. But today's spicy chickpea curry was definitely in Corey's top five. Maybe even top three!

The truth was, the cafeteria food had always

been tasty—lots of burgers, grilled cheese, and more burgers. But lately Mrs. Collins had been trying all sorts of different recipes, and the cafeteria food had gone from good to great. It started earlier this year when Mrs. Collins agreed to try Miss Hodges's recipe for meatless meat loaf—but it made a bunch of kids sick! Everyone was quick to blame Miss Hodges, but Club CSI had investigated the case and cleared Miss Hodges's name. Hannah, Ben, and Corey had solved a few more mysteries since then, each one more surprising than the last. One thing they'd learned right away was that there was no way to know when a mystery was about to unfold.

Suddenly a girl with straight blond hair caught up to Corey, and started walking in step with him.

"Corey," she said breathlessly. "Corey. I've *got* to talk to you."

Corey blinked in surprised. Whitney Martino was the prettiest, most popular girl in eighth grade. He was amazed that she even knew his name. For a second, Corey forgot about rushing to the lunch line . . . but only for a second.

"Uh, sure," Corey replied. "Let's talk in line."

But Whitney shook her head. "In line? With

everybody, like, *listening* to us? No. This is *private*."

"Oh," Corey answered, growing more confused by the second.

"Follow me," Whitney said, wrapping her fingers around Corey's wrist as she pulled him over to the corner. Corey took one last, longing look at the lunch line as Whitney dragged him away. *There will still be a chance to score seconds in a minute*, he assured himself.

"So what's up?" Corey asked.

Whitney glanced around to make sure no one was nearby. "I have a case for you," she said in a dramatic whisper. "A *huge* case. Like, *enormous*."

Corey perked up at once. "Oh, for Club CSI?"

Whitney nodded. "I need to tell you what's been going on. Can you meet me after school at the soccer field?"

"Or we could just talk about it now," Corey suggested. "Do you want to come over to my table? Ben and Hannah are over there—"

"No, no," Whitney said quickly. "No, that won't work. It has to be after school. There can't be a lot of people around."

Corey glanced over at Ben and Hannah, who

were staring at him. He knew that he shouldn't make plans for Club CSI before checking with them first. But Whitney was insistent. And he just knew that Mrs. Collins was going to run out of chickpea curry any second now.

"Okay, fine," Corey finally gave in. "Soccer field. Right after school."

Whitney flashed him a dazzling smile. "Thank you *soooo* much!" she said. "I'll be waiting for you!"

As Corey walked away, he shook his head. He didn't get the way girls acted sometimes. But if Whitney had a case for Club CSI, they would do everything they could to help.

When Corey reached the lunch line, he groaned. It was just as he feared: All the chickpea curry, all the spiced rice, and all the naan bread were gone! The only thing left was a bowl of fruit. With a sigh, Corey grabbed an apple and then paid the cashier. The moment he returned to his table, Hannah pounced.

"Did you just have a conversation with *Whitney Martino*? What did she want? Why was she talking to *you*?"

Corey gave her a look.

"Not that, you know, it's just . . . *Whitney Martino*," Hannah said quickly. "I mean, she doesn't talk to *any* seventh graders. She hardly even speaks to any of the eighth graders."

"She has a case for us," Corey said with a shrug, then took a bite out of his apple. "It sounds like a pretty big deal. I told her we'd meet her at the soccer field right after school."

Now it was Hannah's turn to give Corey a look. "Wait a second. You set up a meeting for Club CSI without asking us?"

Corey took another bite of his apple. "Um . . . yeah. Whitney didn't give me another choice."

Hannah frowned.

"What's the problem?" Corey asked. "The whole point of Club CSI is to help solve crimes that happen at school. Whitney *is* a student here. . . ."

"Look, it's just that Whitney is—" Hannah paused. "What's the best way to explain this? Whitney is . . . Well, you guys know she's the most popular girl at Woodlands, right?"

"Right," Corey and Ben replied.

"But that doesn't mean she's the nicest," Hannah continued in a quieter voice. "And when Whitney wants something . . . well, she'll do just about any-thing to get it."

"I don't know, Hannah," Corey replied as the bell rang. "She seemed pretty nice to me . . . except when she accidentally made me miss out on sec-onds!"

Hannah opened her mouth, but she closed it before saying anything. Then she picked up her lunch tray. "I hope you're right," she replied as she walked over to the trash cans against the wall.

But both Corey and Ben could tell there was something more she wanted to say.

Chapter 2

Just minutes after the final bell rang, Hannah, Ben, and Corey were waiting at the soccer field. There was only one problem: Whitney Martino was nowhere to be found. Five minutes passed, then ten, and then Hannah let out a sigh. "I don't know about you guys, but I think we've waited long enough," she said as she looped her backpack over her arm. "I'll see you guys tomorrow."

"Wait, you're leaving?" Corey asked.

"Yeah," Hannah replied. "No Whitney, no case. No case, no reason to waste the afternoon standing around for no reason. Besides, I have a ton of homework."

"Yeah, and I want my afternoon snack, but we promised Whitney we'd meet her," said Corey.

"I hate to break it to you, Corey," said Hannah, "but I don't think Whitney cares."

Ben checked his watch. "Let's give her a few more minutes," he suggested. "We can start our English reading while we wait."

"All right," Hannah relented. But she didn't look happy about it.

After another ten minutes, Corey finally spotted Whitney sauntering toward them. "Here she comes," he said, nudging Hannah's arm. "Better late than never, right?"

"If you say so," Hannah said under her breath.

"Cor-eeeeeeeeeeeeeeeeeeeeey!" Whitney called out in a singsong voice. "Hey!"

Club CSI waited for Whitney to apologize for being so late. But she just stood there.

"Everything okay?" Corey asked. "I thought we were meeting right after school?"

Whitney shrugged. "I had a cheerleading meeting."

"Cheerleading?" Corey said. "But football and basketball seasons are over."

"Silly!" Whitney cried with a big smile. "Cheerleading isn't just for other sports. We have stuff going on all year. And a *ton* of really important competitions. Regionals are in, like, three weeks! I know we're going to place this year. Have you ever been to one of our meets?"

Corey shook his head.

Whitney flashed him another smile. "Oh, you totally have to come to Regionals!"

Hannah cleared her throat. "Can we talk about your case? I don't mean to be rude; it's just that we've been waiting, well, a long time—"

Whitney looked at Ben and Hannah like she was just noticing that they were there. "So, go ahead and do . . . whatever it is you do. I'm here to meet with *Corey*," she said coolly.

"Whitney, I'm kind of confused," Ben said, frowning. "Corey said you have a problem. Club CSI is ready to help. But we can't help if you won't tell us what's going on."

"We're a team," added Corey.

Whitney looked from Corey to Ben to Hannah and then back to Corey. She finally seemed to realize they were a package deal. "Fine," she said and then leaned in close and whispered, "Someone is out to get me."

"That sounds really serious," Ben replied at once. "Why don't you start from the beginning and tell us everything. Don't leave anything out—even if it seems trivial or unimportant."

"Tell you everything?" repeated Whitney.

"Everything," Corey confirmed.

"Uh . . . it's just, uh, like a feeling I have," Whitney mumbled.

"A feeling?" Hannah asked skeptically.

"Yeah," Whitney said. "I just *know* that someone is plotting something."

"Okay," Corey said slowly. "But, well, why do you think that?"

"Because . . . of my, um, locker. Someone, uh, someone broke into it!" Whitney exclaimed.

"That's awful," Corey said sympathetically. "Was anything stolen?"

"Well . . . no," Whitney admitted.

"Any vandalism?" asked Hannah.

"Was the lock tampered with?" Ben questioned. "Were there any signs of forced entry?"

"Well, you know, no," Whitney said, glancing away from the others. "I mean, maybe. It's, um, hard to tell."

"It's hard to tell if your locker was *broken into*?" Hannah asked skeptically.

"Excuse me," Whitney shot back. "I didn't do anything wrong! Why are you grilling me like this?"

"We're just trying to figure out if a crime has been committed," Ben said calmly.

Whitney turned to Corey. "Will you come to my locker, Corey?" she asked, completely shutting out Ben and Hannah. "So you can, I don't know, finger-print it? Or whatever?"

"See, Whitney, here's the thing," Ben began. "It doesn't sound like a crime has actually happened. Or, at least, there's no evidence of a crime right now, so fingerprinting the locker wouldn't tell us much."

"But if somebody's gross fingerprints are all over my locker—" Whitney argued.

"Honestly, we wouldn't launch an investigation without knowing for certain that something had happened," Ben continued. "But if anything *does* happen—"

"Club CSI will definitely investigate," said Corey, giving Whitney a little reassuring smile.

"Okay, I guess," Whitney said slowly.

"See you later," Corey said as Club CSI turned to

leave. As soon as they were certain that Whitney was out of earshot, Ben and Corey began talking quietly about their strange meeting with the most popular girl at Woodlands Junior High. Hannah, though, took one last glance over her shoulder. Whitney was still standing in the same spot, staring into the distance with her eyes narrowed.

There was something else that Hannah had noticed about Whitney during their conversation: She hadn't made eye contact with *any* of the members of Club CSI when she told them about her locker. Hannah didn't want to read too much into it, but she couldn't help remembering what Miss Hodges had taught them in class earlier that day. And if Whitney was lying about someone breaking into her locker . . . what, exactly, did she want from Club CSI?

Chapter 3

The next morning there was a surprise waiting for Corey at his locker.

Whitney Martino!

"Corey!" she exclaimed. "Someone—someone—someone—"

Corey had never seen a girl this upset before. Her lips were trembling, and even her hands were shaking. "Whoa, whoa, whoa, slow down," he said. "What's wrong, Whitney?"

"Someone broke into my locker!" Whitney cried.

"You're sure?" asked Corey.

Whitney nodded emphatically. "Yes. Absolutely. It happened! I know it! Someone broke into my locker and vandalized it!"

"Oh man," Corey replied. "I'm so sorry, Whitney.

This is definitely Club CSI territory. Go wait by your locker—I'll be right there."

"Thank you," Whitney said. Her voice even wavered a bit as though she was about to cry.

Corey ran down the hall to get Hannah and Ben. "Guys. Someone definitely broke into Whitney's locker and vandalized it," he reported. "I told her we would come check it out before class."

"Wow, I guess her suspicions were right," Ben said. He zipped open the inside pouch of his backpack to make sure he had some standard investigation supplies: rubber gloves, tweezers, and small plastic bags for holding evidence.

Club CSI hurried through the hallway toward Whitney's locker. They stopped in front of it and stared.

"Am I missing something?" Hannah asked Ben in a low voice. "Her locker looks fine to me."

"Yeah, the outside does," Whitney snapped as she walked up behind them. She pushed past Hannah and Ben, then twirled the lock and opened the door.

"Thanks for rushing over here so quickly, Corey," Whitney said sweetly as the members of Club CSI tried to get a good look inside her locker.

"Uh, you're welcome," said Corey. He wasn't sure,

but he thought maybe his face turned slightly pink.

At first glance, things seemed fine inside Whitney's locker too. Every surface of her locker was decorated. It had a sparkly minichandelier swinging from the top and a shaggy hot-pink rug at the bottom. There was a mirror covered in pink glitter and a notepad where Whitney's friends left her notes like "U R THE BEST, WHIT!" The locker's walls were crowded with photos of Whitney, the cheerleading squad, and all her friends. It wasn't easy for Club CSI to immediately spot the vandalism through all the clutter.

But when Whitney pointed at a photo of herself and her best friend, Alyssa, the vandalism was obvious to everyone. Someone had drawn all over Whitney's face with a marker, using it to black out her teeth, give her a shaggy beard, and even add a pig's snout over her nose.

"Who would do something like this?" Whitney asked dramatically. "This is the *worst* thing that's ever happened to me!"

Club CSI secretly thought Whitney was overreacting a little, but they would treat the case as seriously as any other.

"Whitney, do you mind if I take some photos of your locker?" Hannah asked as she pulled out her cell phone. "It's important to document the crime scene exactly as it was found."

Whitney shook her head.

Ben pulled on a pair of gloves. "Let me take a look at the lock," he said, peering at it as he spun the dial a few times. Ben remembered what Club CSI had learned about locks on another case, when they had interviewed a locksmith. Ben guessed that a metal combination lock like the one embedded in Whitney's locker would be hard to pick, and he was right.

"I don't see any signs of obvious tampering," Ben told the others. "I'm guessing whoever did this either knew, or guessed, your combination. But I'll come back to fingerprint your locker after school. There's just not time to do it now."

"Can't Corey do that?" Whitney asked.

"If you need fingerprinting, Ben is your guy," Corey said quickly. "He's really good at it."

"Oh yeah?" Whitney asked. She gave Corey a little smile. "What's your specialty, Corey? Besides being a great football player."

Corey looked down at his feet. "Um, I guess I

kind of have a way with people," he said, trying not to brag. "So I usually take the lead in interviews."

"Oh, I can definitely see that," said Whitney. "You're the coolest guy in the seventh grade."

Hannah rolled her eyes. "Speaking of having a way with people," she said loudly, "Whitney, do you know of anyone at school who might have a problem with you? Anyone who might want to do something like this?"

"Nope. Nobody," Whitney said.

Hannah gave her a pointed look. "Nobody? Really? Are you sure about that?"

"Absolutely sure," Whitney replied firmly, finally facing Hannah. "Maybe you missed it, but I was just voted Most Popular—*again*."

"Does anybody know the combination to your locker?" Ben jumped in.

"Yeah," Whitney said slowly. "My best friend, Alyssa, does. But she would *never, ever* do anything like this. Ever. I mean, she's the one who gave me that picture." She seemed distracted by Corey, who was scribbling something in his notebook. "What are you writing down?"

Corey glanced up. "Just making some notes for

when I interview Alyssa later," he explained.

"But I just told you that she wouldn't do this," Whitney said. "There's, like, no reason for you to interview her. I really don't want you talking to her."

Corey frowned. "But the interviews are—"

"Come *on*, Corey! I don't want you talking to her! Why is that a problem?" demanded Whitney.

"How about *I* interview Alyssa?" Hannah asked.

"Yeah. Let her do it," Whitney said at once. "And then you guys can meet me here after school. For the fingerprinting."

Just then the bell rang. It was time for homeroom. Whitney slammed her locker shut, spun the dial, and then lifted the latch—just to make sure it was really locked.

"So it sounds like we have a plan," Ben said as he peeled off his gloves. "Whitney, try not to use your locker until after we've dusted for prints. We'll meet back here after school." Then he paused and glanced at Whitney. "*Right* after school."

For a minute, Whitney looked like she was about to say something snarky. But instead she simply nodded her head and walked off to homeroom.

Chapter 4

Despite Whitney's assurances that she would be on time, Ben and Corey expected her to be late again when they met her at her locker after school. But they were wrong. This time, Whitney was waiting for *them*, leaning against the long row of lockers like there was nowhere else she'd rather be.

"Hey, Corey," Whitney said with her usual dazzling smile. Then she glanced over toward Ben and said, "Hey . . ." It was almost as if she'd forgotten his name.

"So I didn't use my locker for the whole rest of the day," Whitney continued. "Just like you asked."

"Great," said Ben. "I want to check inside your locker for any evidence, but first let me dust the outside and lock for fingerprints."

Corey watched as Ben got to work, and Whitney watched Corey. "So, Corey," Whitney began, "thanks so much for helping me. You're the best."

"No problem," Corey replied. "Club CSI is always happy to help a fellow student."

"I'm thinking of having a party in a few weeks," Whitney added. "You'll definitely be invited."

"Oh" was all Corey said in response. There was an awkward silence before Ben stood up.

"All right. I found a print and a partial on the lock. I'll analyze them later." Ben gestured toward the lock. "Do you mind opening it up for me, Whitney?"

Whitney spun the dial to enter her combination and then swung open her locker door. Ben stared into her locker, frowning, as he tried to figure out the best plan of action. He had a feeling Whitney wouldn't be happy to see him cover the inside of her locker with black and white dusting powder.

Finally, Ben decided to check the metal edges of the locker door next—the one surface Whitney hadn't decorated. He thought there was a good chance that the vandal might have touched the edge of the door to open it. Ben carefully dipped his brush into the container of black powder and dusted it over the surface.

Whitney seemed supremely uninterested in Ben's fingerprinting process.

"So I was thinking," she said to Corey. "After? When this is all done? We could go get something to eat."

"Just a sec," Corey said, stepping forward to take a picture of any prints that appeared under the dust.

"Hey, you know, there's something about that photo . . . ," Ben mused, looking at the photo that had been drawn on.

Whitney's laugh was forced. "What? How spectacularly hideous it makes me look?"

Ben shook his head. "The tape!" he suddenly exclaimed. "I bet we'll find the vandal's prints on the tape!"

"What—what are you talking about?" Whitney asked. She looked pale.

"Well, obviously the photo was moved at some point," Ben explained. "You can tell how hard it would be to draw on it from this angle. So the vandal must have taken it down, drawn on it, and then taped it back up. That's my theory, anyway. And if I'm right, we could find the vandal's prints on the tape!"

"Good thinking, Ben," Corey said approvingly.

But Whitney frowned. Her eyes darted off to the side. "Look, I just—I, um, I really don't think that the vandal took down the picture. I mean, this is, uh, my locker, you know? I, uh, I look at that picture every day. I would know if *it* had been moved."

"But we should check, anyway," Ben insisted. "Just in case."

Whitney pressed her lips into a thin line, but she didn't argue as Ben slowly removed the photo from the inside of her locker.

"Yes!" Ben exclaimed as examined the tape. "Check it out—one complete, perfect fingerprint! We'll definitely be able to analyze this in the lab." He peeled off the piece of tape from the photo and secured it so that the print wouldn't smudge.

Then Corey pulled an ink pad out of the fingerprinting kit. "And, of course, we need to get your fingerprints," he told Whitney.

Her fists clenched. "Why? *I* didn't do it," she said in a rush.

Ben and Corey looked at each other. "No one said that," Ben replied. "But since it's your locker, your prints will be all over it. So we need your prints to make sure the ones we've lifted don't belong to you."

"Oh. I get it," Whitney said. She let Corey press her fingertips onto the ink pad, then make a clear print from each finger on a plain white card. Afterward, Corey gave her an alcohol swab to remove the ink from her hands.

"I guess we're done for now," Ben said as he packed up the fingerprinting kit.

Whitney turned to Corey. "So, how about it?" she asked him. "You want to get something to eat? Some ice cream?"

"Ice cream. That sounds awesome," Corey replied. Now that he thought about it, his stomach had been grumbling for his afternoon snack.

Ben shot Corey a look. If they were going to solve this case quickly, they needed to analyze the evidence today.

Corey got the hint. "But no, thanks, Whitney. Normally, I definitely would, but we've got to ana-lyze these prints. And find out how Hannah's inter-view went."

"Oh," said Whitney.

"We'll be in touch as soon as we know more," Ben

promised. "And hopefully the vandal won't strike again—but if they do, text me right away. Or Corey. Or Hannah."

Whitney took out her phone, and Ben recited each of their numbers. He wasn't positive, but it seemed like Whitney only typed in Corey's number.

Next, Ben and Corey went straight to the lab attached to Miss Hodges's classroom to analyze the prints. Hannah was already there, waiting for them.

"Hey, guys. How did the fingerprinting go?" she asked.

"Pretty good," Ben replied. "We even picked up a print from the tape attached to the vandalized photo!"

"Nice work!" Hannah said. Then she pushed a card across the counter. "Since I was interviewing Alyssa, I got her fingerprints, too."

"So you think she's a suspect?" asked Corey.

Hannah shook her head. "Actually, no. But since she knows Whitney's locker combo, I figured Alyssa's prints might be on it. At least this will help us rule them out."

"How did the interview go?" Ben said.

"It was kind of tough," Hannah replied. "Alyssa

was really upset and distracted. It was hard to keep her focused. She thought Corey should be interviewing her. I swear, she must have mentioned it four different times."

Corey looked surprised. "Seriously? Are you for real?" he asked as a grin spread across his face. "I can't believe the whole school is talking about my interview skills! Word is really getting around."

"Maybe," Hannah said. "But, anyway, back to the interview. Alyssa admitted that she knows the combination to Whitney's locker, but she completely denies doing anything to the photo. And you know what? I believe her."

"How come?" asked Ben.

"Well, I know I don't have Corey's amazing interview skills," Hannah joked, "but I still observed her very carefully. She maintained eye contact with me the whole time, and she never stuttered or stammered or fidgeted or anything. And I also—I just have a *feeling*, you know? And I think that counts for something."

"It definitely does," Ben said. He moved back from the microscope. "Anybody else want to take a look at these prints?"

Hannah peered into the microscope first, then Corey had a turn. "Lots of smudges and partials," Corey observed.

"Yes. And these ones from the locker door are clearly Whitney's, which is to be expected," Ben said. "What do you think about the print from the tape?"

Hannah looked into the microscope again. "I'd say that's Whitney's print too," she replied.

"Now, I was able to lift a few prints from the photo itself," Ben continued. "Whitney's prints are obvious—again, that's to be expected—but check this one out. The whorl is pretty different."

The swirly lines on that fingerprint were obviously different from Whitney's prints. Hannah picked up the piece of paper where she had had Alyssa stamp her fingerprint and then compared the two. "It matches Alyssa's fingerprint," she said. "But that doesn't mean anything, really. Since Alyssa gave the photo to Whitney, her prints would be all over it."

The three friends were silent for a moment. Then Hannah spoke again. "Guys, I think this case is a waste of time," she said.

"No," Ben disagreed. "I mean, *someone* vandalized that photo. And we shouldn't quit until we've figured out who. What's next? Will someone graffiti the outside of Whitney's locker? Or perhaps steal some of the decorations from inside?"

"Hopefully not, of course," Hannah said. "But unless something else happens . . . the trail is cold, right?" She turned to Corey. "You've been pretty quiet. What do you think we should do next?"

Corey shrugged. "You both made good points," he said. "So I think we should wait and see if the vandal strikes again . . . or if any other clues turn up."

Ben and Hannah could both agree on that.

Chapter 5

Before school the next day, Hannah intercepted Corey on the way to his locker. "Come on, let's go find Ben," she said. "I had an idea last night—about Whitney's case."

Corey was surprised. "Really? You seemed so ready to stop working on it."

"I know," Hannah admitted. "But Ben's right. *Someone* vandalized that photo—and if the only prints we have are Whitney's and Alyssa's, then at the very least we should re-interview them, right? *Both* of them, I mean. And you should be the one to do it."

As Corey puffed up with pride, they arrived at Ben's locker. Though Ben's face was twisted into an unusual scowl, Hannah jumped right in with her new plan. "So . . . Whitney's case—" she began.

"Forget it. You were right," Ben said bluntly. "Total waste of time."

Corey and Hannah stared at him in surprise. "Um, who are you and what have you done with Ben?" Corey joked. "Ben would never say that about an open investigation!"

"What changed your mind?" Hannah asked.

Ben paused, as if he wasn't sure he wanted to say. But he knew he couldn't keep this a secret from Club CSI. It wouldn't be fair to Hannah and Corey. Without another word, he pulled a crumpled-up piece of paper out of his backpack.

"Alyssa found me on my way into school this morning, and she gave me this," he said in a quiet voice. "Just . . . read it for yourselves."

To: MissLys@we-mail.com

From: cheergirl12@smartmail.com

Sent: Wednesday, April 4, 4:56 p.m.

Subject: Club CSI—LOSERS!!!

Lys! OMG, I am soooo soooo soooo sorry u had 2 deal with Club

CSI 2day. What a bunch of dorks! Seriously, I am always 5 secs from falling asleep when they R around. I don't even care who broke in2 my locker anymore. Like those losers could even figure it out. I'm surprised they figured out how 2 tie their shoes! LOL. Their "investigation" was so incredibly dumb. If they try 2 talk 2 u again, just ignore them and hopefully they will go away!!!

<3

whit

When Hannah finished reading, she glanced up at Ben with a knowing look in her eye. "You seem surprised," she said. "And upset."

"Well, aren't you?" he asked. "Whitney came to *us*. I don't know why she'd send such a mean e-mail to Alyssa. We were only trying to help. Because she asked us to!"

Ben reached out for the e-mail, but Corey

snatched it away from him. Then he turned and stormed off down the hall. Ben and Hannah had to run after him just to keep up.

Corey marched over to Whitney, who was staring at her reflection in her locker mirror. "You owe us an explanation," he said hotly. "And an apology."

Whitney jumped and spun around to face Corey. "Huh?" she asked. "What?"

"Don't pretend you don't know," Corey snapped as he shoved the e-mail toward her.

As Whitney read the e-mail, her face fell into a troubled frown. When she looked up again, her eyes were open wide. "I—I didn't send this e-mail," she stammered.

"Yeah, right," Corey said sarcastically.

"No, Corey, I mean it," Whitney said, staring directly into his eyes. "I don't understand—I mean, that's definitely my e-mail address, but I *know* I didn't send the e-mail. I couldn't have. I was in ballet class yesterday from four to five."

"So if you didn't send it . . . ," Hannah began slowly.

"Someone must have broken into my e-mail account!" Whitney finished for her. She looked from

Hannah to Ben to Corey. Corey still looked upset.

"Corey, please, you have to believe me. I would never call you a loser," Whitney said so sincerely that everyone believed her. "Whoever wrote this e-mail . . . it wasn't me. I swear."

Corey looked at Whitney and nodded. She did sound very sincere, and she hadn't been anything but nice to him since coming up to him in the cafeteria.

"So do you want us to continue with our investigation?" Hannah asked, just to be sure.

Whitney nodded. "Yes. Please," she said. "It totally freaks me out that someone sent that e-mail from my account."

"And broke into your locker," Ben added.

"Huh? Oh. Yeah, of course," she said.

Hannah, Ben, and Corey walked away from Whitney's locker in a tight little group so that no one could overhear their conversation. "We need to interview Alyssa again," Corey said right away. "And this time, we should *all* be there."

As luck would have it, Club CSI passed Alyssa on their way back to the seventh-grade hallway. She had just purchased a protein bar from a vending machine when Hannah tapped her on the shoulder.

"Oh. Hey. What's up?" Alyssa asked.

"Can we talk to you for a minute?" asked Hannah.

"About what?" Alyssa sounded bored.

"I think you know," Ben replied.

Alyssa raised an eyebrow, but she didn't argue as Club CSI led her toward an empty classroom. Once inside, Corey put the crumpled printout of Alyssa's e-mail on a desk.

"What can you tell us about this?" he asked.

"This?" Alyssa asked. She tucked a strand of her long auburn hair behind her ear, then started twirling it around her finger. "This is the e-mail—the one I gave Ben before school."

"Why?" Corey asked. "If your best friend sent you this e-mail in private, why would you show it to Ben?"

Alyssa shrugged and glanced over Corey's shoulder, toward the door. "Just, you know . . . I thought you guys should know. What Whitney really thinks about you."

"Do you usually print out her e-mails and show them to people?" Hannah asked.

"Do I usually what?" Alyssa frowned. She started

chewing on her cuticles. "I don't know what you're getting at, but you should be thanking me. Whitney was trashing you guys behind your back. I thought you'd want to know. *I* certainly would."

"Here's the thing," Ben began. "We showed this e-mail to Whitney, and she says that she didn't send it."

"You did *what*?" Alyssa blurted out. "Look, I don't have time for this. I wouldn't have even shown it to you if I'd known you'd turn it into such a big deal. Just forget it, okay?"

Then Alyssa picked her up bag and hurried toward the door.

"Hang on," Corey called after her. "We have a few more questions we want to—"

But she was already gone.

"Well, *that* was weird," Hannah remarked.

"So she didn't act like that when you interviewed her yesterday?" Corey asked.

"No. Not at all," Hannah replied. "She didn't fidget, and she just seemed a lot more . . . I don't know. Less nervous, I guess."

"Maybe she's worried that Whitney will get mad at her for showing me the e-mail," Ben suggested.

"Or maybe it's because somebody used Whitney's e-mail account to contact her," Corey said.

"Or maybe it's just something else altogether," Hannah said as the bell rang.

After forensic science, Hannah excused herself from the usual dash to the cafeteria with Ben and Corey. Her two best friends had already started eating by the time she hurried into the cafeteria and sat down at their usual table, her face flushed.

"I have news," she said. "It might be important for our case."

"What's up?" Ben asked.

"Whitney and Alyssa had a fight this morning," Hannah reported. "Everybody in the girls' bathroom was talking about it, so I hung around to listen. It happened just before homeroom, right after we spoke to Alyssa. And when I say 'fight,' I mean *huge* fight. Enormous. Maybe even bigger than the one they had with Maya."

Corey and Ben looked confused. "Maya?" Corey repeated.

"You guys don't know about that?" Hannah asked.

"It was the biggest drama at Woodlands last year."

Ben shrugged. "Sorry. I don't know anything about this."

"Let me fill you in," Hannah said. "So, up until last year, Maya, Alyssa, and Whitney were totally inseparable. They did *everything* together. They even coordinated their outfits every night before they went to bed. But then Alyssa and Maya both started crushing on Scott Leesom, and they had a big fight over who liked him first, and Whitney took Alyssa's side. They started ignoring Maya, and she was totally *crushed*. And practically friendless for the rest of the year. She even quit the cheerleading squad over it."

"Wow! Why didn't you mention this before?" Ben asked. "Maya should be treated as a suspect. She definitely has motive, right?"

Corey rubbed his hands together. "Dude, I cannot *wait* to interview her."

"Wait, guys," Hannah spoke up. "There's no way Maya vandalized the photo. She's been out of school all week because her uncle is getting married in Mexico on Saturday, and her whole family went down early to help with the wedding preparations."

"How do you know all this?" Ben asked in amazement.

Hannah shrugged. "You can find out a lot in the girls' room," she said matter-of-factly.

"It is possible she hacked into Whitney's e-mail from Mexico," Corey pointed out. "We should still interview her when she gets back."

"But how would she know about the investigation if she's been absent for the entire week?" Hannah asked.

"Maybe someone else e-mailed her about it?" Corey suggested. But he didn't sound convinced.

"I guess it's possible. And we can certainly interview her when she gets back. But I think we should find out more about Whitney and Alyssa's fight," replied Hannah. "Because, really, why did Alyssa show you that e-mail, Ben? That was a major betrayal of her best friend. It doesn't add up."

"You're right," Ben said. "It doesn't. So the most important thing to do now is figure out who sent the e-mail."

"I know what that means," Corey spoke up. "Our investigation is about to go digital!"

Chapter 6

Right after school, Club CSI decided to check out Whitney's alibi. It wouldn't be hard to confirm that she really was in ballet class when the e-mail was sent, since Hannah and Whitney took lessons at the same ballet studio, Pirouette. They weren't in the same class, but they had the same teacher, Miss Yvette.

"What if Whitney sent the e-mail from her phone?" Ben asked as they walked together.

"Not possible," Hannah replied. "Cell phones are definitely not allowed at Pirouette. Miss Yvette *freaks* if somebody's cell goes off during a lesson."

"Really?" Corey asked curiously. "What does she do? Throw ballet slippers? Shred tutus? Tear ribbons with her teeth?"

"Believe me, it's not pretty." And that was all Hannah would say on the subject.

When they arrived at Pirouette, Hannah checked her watch. "Miss Yvette will be in a lesson for fifteen more minutes," she told the boys. "But we can just hang out in the lobby until she's free."

The lobby was nearly empty, except for a teenage girl who was kneeling next to a wall. She was surrounded by open bottles of paint in vibrant, shimmery colors. She looked up as the silver bell on the door chimed.

Hannah waved at the girl. "Hey, Jessica, how's it going?" she asked in a low voice so she wouldn't accidentally disrupt the lesson.

"Hey, Hannah! Are you taking lessons on Thursdays now?" Jessica asked.

Hannah shook her head. "No, just Saturday mornings—at least until summer vacation starts," she said. She turned to Ben and Corey. "Jessica is the most talented dancer at Pirouette."

Corey and Ben looked impressed, but Jessica seemed a little embarrassed. "I just really love dancing, that's all," she said modestly. Then she waved her paintbrush in the air. "And painting, of course!"

"Did you do all this?" Ben asked, gesturing at the wall, where a sprawling mural had been sketched. In the mural, ballerinas danced through an enchanted forest, with rainbow-colored ribbons streaming behind them.

"Guilty," Jessica said with a grin. Then she turned back to the wall so that she could keep painting as she talked. "I finally finished sketching last weekend. It's so great to start adding color and see it come to life!"

"These poses are amazing," Hannah said. "So realistic!"

"You think?" Jessica asked, pleased. "I guess I've been able to observe a lot of dancers, since I take lessons five days a week with Miss Yvette and have solo practice in the studio the other two days. When Miss Yvette offered me extra lessons in exchange for painting the mural, I was like, 'Absolutely!' I mean, I practically live here, anyway!"

Club CSI laughed. Then Ben had an idea.

"So, were you here yesterday?" he asked Jessica.

"Yes, until five o'clock," she replied. "That's when Pirouette closes."

Hannah understood right away why Ben had

asked that question. "Do you remember if Whitney was in class yesterday?" she said.

Jessica stopped to think. Then she nodded. "Intermediate ballet, Wednesdays, four o'clock to five o'clock. She was definitely here," Jessica replied. "I remember because she thought that the dancer over there with the purple tiara looked like her."

"Of course she did," Hannah said with a grin. "Thanks, Jessica. See you Saturday?"

"Absolutely," Jessica said. "If I'm not pirouetting, I'll be painting!"

Once they were on the sidewalk waiting for the bus that would take them close to their homes, Club CSI immediately started talking about the case again. "So Whitney's alibi checks out," Hannah said. "I have to admit, I'm a little surprised."

"How come you hate her so much?" asked Corey bluntly.

"I don't *hate* her," Hannah replied. "It's just that she's notorious for being kind of mean, especially to kids in lower grades. So when I read a mean e-mail sent from her account, I assume Whitney is the one who sent it."

"Do you guys have your Quark Pads with you?" Ben interrupted them.

Hannah and Corey shook their heads. A while back, each member of Club CSI had received a Quark Pad as a reward for uncovering a ring of thieves who had been stealing the electronic tablets and selling them to kids. But because Quark Pads were really expensive, the club members usually didn't bring them to school unless they knew that they would need them.

"Me neither," Ben said as a bus pulled up and Club CSI got on it. "Too bad. Anyway, let's go over to my house. I think our next step should be tracing the e-mail's IP address."

Corey and Hannah looked at him in confusion. "The e-mail's what-what?" Corey asked.

"IP address," Ben repeated. "It stands for 'Internet protocol address.' Basically, every computer connected to the Internet has its own unique IP address—a long string of numbers. It's how computers communicate with websites and stuff."

"So what does that mean for us?" Hannah said.

"If you can find the IP address for certain computer functions—say, sending an e-mail—sometimes you can trace it to find out which computer was used," Ben explained. "Earlier today, I was able to find the IP address for the e-mail Alyssa received. Hopefully, our luck will continue and we'll be able to find out which computer was used to send it."

"You mean we could find out the sender's address?" Corey asked excitedly. "Then the case would be solved, right?"

"Perhaps," Ben said. "If the e-mail was sent from a public computer, like at school or a café, it will get a little trickier. Either way, it will still give us more info than we have now."

"How'd you get the IP address, anyway?" Hannah said. "I don't remember seeing any long numbers on that printout."

"I needed digital access to the e-mail itself," Ben said. "So I asked Whitney to log on to her e-mail at school and let me see the copy that was in her sent folder. The IP address was hidden, but I know this website that will uncover them."

"That's cool . . . and a little creepy," Hannah admitted. "It's sort of freaky to think that there are all these secret records on the Internet, huh?"

"You'd be surprised how many records there are,"

Ben said as they arrived at his house. Since his parents weren't home yet, Ben unlocked the front door. Corey made a beeline for the kitchen. For once, he was actually happy he waited for his afternoon snack. Ben's mom always had the best cookies. Once Corey felt he had sufficiently crammed enough cookies into his mouth, he joined his friends in Ben's room, which was the perfect place for analyzing evidence outside of school. Thanks to Ben's love of everything having to do with science, he had plenty of chemistry sets, dissection kits, and science books. Ben even had his three microscopes! He powered up his computer then and opened his Internet browser.

"Check out this site," Ben said "All you have to do is enter the IP address and . . . Bam! It plots it on a map."

Hannah and Corey leaned over his shoulders to get a better look at the screen. "Um, Corey?" Ben began, turning to his still-munching friend. "You're getting crumbs all over my keyboard."

"Oh sorry," said Corey. "I guess it couldn't hurt to hold the cookies over a napkin."

"Yeah," said Ben, and then he made a little joke. "I've got enough cookies *inside* my computer already."

When Corey and Hannah didn't laugh, Ben continued. "You know, cookies. Information from the Internet that gets stored on your hard drive? Digital markers that track sites you've visited on the Internet?"

"Oh yeah. I've heard of those," said Hannah. And then she smiled. "Do you think we can get back to the map now?"

Ben entered the IP address from the e-mail.

"I guess this rules out Maya," Hannah said as a map of their town appeared on the screen. "The e-mail was sent locally, wasn't it?"

"It looks that way," Ben replied, nodding.

"Zoom in!" Corey cried as a blinking red arrow appeared over the map.

Ben clicked the mouse until a street address flashed on to the map: 1250 Oak Street.

"So is that it? Is that the sender's address?" Corey asked.

"We're about to find out," Ben replied as he ran an Internet search on the address.

For a moment, no one spoke as Club CSI stared at the search results.

"Well, that can't be right," Hannah finally said.

"The library isn't on Oak Street. It's on Westwood."

"I think . . . ," Ben said slowly, "I think this is the address for the new branch. The one that opened a few months ago."

Corey grabbed his backpack. "What are we waiting for?" he asked. "Let's go!"

Chapter 7

Ben, Hannah, and Corey ran to the street corner, where they caught a bus across town to the new branch of the library.

"I wish we had known we'd be going to the new library when we were still at Pirouette," Corey said. "It's just a few blocks away from there, isn't it?"

"Yeah. I can't believe I haven't been there yet," replied Hannah. "I'm excited to check it out. I heard it's really cool."

"Me too," Corey replied. "Too bad it isn't closer to school."

"And too bad the e-mail was sent from a public computer," Ben added, still focused on the case.

When they reached the library, the friends spent a few minutes wandering around to get acquainted with the layout. Tall rows of bookshelves filled with brand-new books lined the walls. The very center of the room had a bank of six computer stations, each one nestled into a unique cubicle. As Club CSI walked around the computers, Ben noticed something. "Look," he whispered to Hannah and Corey. "Each computer's IP address is taped to its monitor! We'll be able to find the exact computer that was used to send the e-mail!"

"That's great and all," Corey whispered back, "but how will that help us find the *person* who sent it?"

"I'm not sure," Ben admitted. "Let's see what we can find out from the librarian."

Hannah glanced over toward the reference desk—and her eyes grew wide. She immediately grabbed Ben's and Corey's shoulders and pulled them behind a row of books.

"Did you guys see that?" she asked in a hushed voice. "The librarian?"

Ben and Corey tried to look, but Hannah pulled them behind the books again.

"It's Alyssa's *mom*!" she said. "Mrs. Gomez. Remember? She subbed in the school library last year when Mrs. Davies had her appendix removed."

"Oh yeah," Ben said as he recognized her.

"What are the odds?" Corey mused. "I mean, this can't be a coincidence, can it?"

"Sure, it can," Ben replied. "Let's go talk to her and see what we can find out."

"Corey, can I take the lead on this interview?" Hannah asked. "I think Mrs. Gomez might remember me. She was really helpful when I was doing research for my report on mummies."

"Yeah, of course," Corey told her.

Hannah approached the reference desk, with Corey and Ben trailing behind her.

"Hey, Mrs. Gomez!" she exclaimed, and then she whispered, "Oops! Sorry to be loud. I'm surprised to see you here!"

Mrs. Gomez smiled warmly at Hannah. "Hi, Hannah," she replied. "How've you been? I miss subbing at the middle school, but when I was offered a full-time job at the brand-new library, I couldn't refuse!"

"It's really nice here," Hannah said. "This is my first time at the new branch."

"Would you like a tour?"

"Oh, we're just kind of . . . exploring on our own,"

said Hannah. She glanced around. "Hey, is Alyssa here?"

Mrs. Gomez shook her head. "No, not today— cheerleading practice."

"Oh," Hannah said slowly. "I thought maybe she would be hanging out here."

"Most days she does," Mrs. Gomez said. "She gets her homework done, and then she likes to use the computer while I finish up. But starting today, she has cheerleading every afternoon until Regionals. Want me to give her a message?"

"Yeah, just tell her I said hi," Hannah said. "I'd probably better get started on my homework too. See you later, Mrs. Gomez."

"Come by and visit me any time!" Mrs. Gomez said with a big smile.

Club CSI didn't talk about the case until they were outside, waiting for the bus.

"Well?" Hannah asked the guys. "What do you think?"

"I don't know," Ben replied. "It's not definitive proof, you know? Just because Alyssa's mom works at the library and Alyssa hangs out there doesn't mean Alyssa sent that e-mail."

"But she's the best suspect we have right now," Corey pointed out.

Hannah pulled her cell phone out of her pocket. "I have an idea," she said. She started texting furiously.

whitney r u there?

"Wait a second," Corey interrupted Hannah. "Whitney must have cheerleading practice too. So you'd better be careful what you text her, since she'll probably be with Alyssa."

"Not unless they made up from their fight," Hannah replied, her eyes glued to her phone. "And that's pretty unlikely. From what I heard, it was *epic*."

Ping!

Corey and Ben squeezed in so they could read Whitney's text along with Hannah.

cheer just ended. what's up?

Hannah sent a quick response.

> quick q. does alyssa know
> your e-mail password?

There was a long pause before Whitney replied.

> yeah . . . y?

Hannah smiled at the response, but she needed to talk to Whitney face-to-face . . . and she knew just how to make that happen. She sent another text.

> just wondering. corey
> has a msg 4 u—can u meet
> us @ his locker tmrw b4
> school?

"Hey, wait," Corey said in a rush. "Why'd you say that?"

"Oh, don't worry," Hannah said as she sent yet

another text. "I'm going to tell Alyssa the same thing."

"But why a message from me?" Corey repeated.

Hannah finally looked up from her phone. "Because I want to make sure they both show up."

Corey went out of his way to arrive at school extra early—but Whitney and Alyssa still beat him. He found the feuding friends waiting for him at his locker . . . and they didn't look very happy about it.

"What's *she* doing here?" both girls snapped at the same time.

"Uh . . . ," Corey stammered. He glanced around wildly, hoping to spot Ben or Hannah. But they were nowhere to be seen. "Uh . . . why don't we just, uh . . ."

Corey grabbed his cell phone and sent an urgent text to Hannah and Ben.

WHERE R U GUYS?!?!!?!

Ping! Ping!

Corey sighed in relief as two text message alerts sounded just behind him. He spun around to see Ben and Hannah turning the corner.

"Hey, guys," Corey said loudly. "Nice of you to join us. Uh, Whitney and Alyssa have been waiting, so—"

"Hi, everyone," Hannah said cheerfully. She turned to Whitney and Alyssa. "We think we've solved the mystery of who really sent that e-mail to Alyssa."

"Oh yeah?" Whitney said, perking up right away. "Well? Who did it? Who hacked my account?"

"We think it was . . . Alyssa," Ben replied.

Club CSI watched Alyssa closely. She opened and closed her mouth very quickly, but no words came out.

"We know that the e-mail was sent from the Oak Street branch of the library—the same one where Alyssa's mom works. We also know it was sent on Wednesday afternoon, at 4:56 p.m., when Alyssa was still hanging out at the library—and using one of the computers. And we also know Alyssa had access to Whitney's e-mail account, since she had the password," Ben continued. "Alyssa, did you send yourself that e-mail from Whitney's account?"

Two tears spilled down Alyssa's cheeks. "Yes," she whispered. "I did."

"*Why* would you do that?" Whitney exploded. "I *cannot* even *believe* you did that!"

Alyssa sniffed loudly and wiped her eyes. She seemed too upset to speak.

"I think I know why," Hannah spoke up. "It's because Alyssa also vandalized the photo in Whitney's locker. You didn't want Club CSI to figure out you were the vandal, so you sent that e-mail hoping we'd get mad at Whitney and drop the case."

"No!" Alyssa cried. "I swear, I didn't touch the photo!" She turned to face Whitney. "You have to believe me, Whit, I would *never* do that."

Whitney looked down at the floor. "I know you didn't," she mumbled.

"How do you know that?" said Corey.

"Because *I* did it, okay?" Whitney snapped. Her face started to turn red. "I scribbled on the picture myself."

Alyssa started to giggle through her tears. "You did that?" she asked Whitney. "You seriously did that?"

A reluctant smile crept across Whitney's face. "I know, right? So lame! I am so embarrassed!" she exclaimed.

Ben and Corey looked completely confused, but a knowing look crossed Hannah's face.

"Did we miss something?" Ben asked her.

Hannah nodded. "Let me guess," she said to Whitney. "You wanted to hang out with Corey . . . so you vandalized the photo to have a reason to talk to him."

Whitney nodded without speaking.

"And you didn't like that," Hannah said to Alyssa, "because . . . you also wanted to hang out with Corey, right?"

Alyssa nodded too.

"So you sent that nasty e-mail to make sure Corey wouldn't want to hang out with Whitney anymore," Hannah finished.

This time, Alyssa covered her face with her hands before nodding. Hannah thought Whitney was going to be really angry. After all, Alyssa tried to sabotage Whitney's plans to get to know Corey. Instead Whitney burst out laughing. "That is the craziest thing you've ever done, Lys," she said.

When Alyssa dropped her hands, she was laughing too. "Yes, but is it crazier than what you did?" she asked. "I don't think so."

"No," Whitney admitted. "Probably not. I am the worst friend. I'm sorry I scribbled on the picture you gave me."

"*I'm* the worst friend! I'm sorry I sent that stupid e-mail from your account," Alyssa apologized.

"F and F?" Whitney asked, holding out her pinkie.

"F and F," Alyssa said, linking her pinkie finger with Whitney's.

Then the two girls hurried down the hall toward the girls' bathroom, their heads bent close together as they whispered something in secret.

"F and F?" Ben said at last. "What does that mean?"

"Oh, that's their little code," Hannah said. "It stands for 'forgive and forget.' This might not surprise you, but Whitney and Alyssa get into a lot of fights. Usually not as big as this one, though."

"But . . . if they wanted to hang out with me, why didn't they just say so?" Corey asked. "Why go to the trouble to make up a case and send fake e-mails and all that stuff?"

"Because they, well, *like* you, Corey," Hannah told him. "I mean, *like* like. You know?"

"Ohhhhhh!" Corey exclaimed as he suddenly understood. Then his face fell a little. "So they weren't just impressed with Club CSI because of my great interviewing skills?"

"I'm sure that had something to do with it," Hannah comforted her friend.

"I guess you were right all along, Hannah," Ben said. "This case pretty much was a waste of time."

She shrugged. "I don't know about that," Hannah replied. "All that IP address stuff was really interesting. And who knows? Maybe it will be useful for another case."

Club CSI had no idea how right Hannah was going to be.

club csi! need help—
URGENT. can u meet me @
my locker after school
tmrw? pls pls pls pls
pls!

Hannah, Ben, and Corey didn't know what to make of the next text message they received from Whitney. It had been a few weeks since they'd solved the Case of the Feuding Friends, which was their unofficial name for what had happened between Whitney and Alyssa, and since then, Whitney and Alyssa had been supertight. Sometimes the girls nodded at Club CSI when they passed them in the halls, but that was about it. It almost seemed like the vandalized photo, the fake e-mail, and their mutual crush on Corey had never even happened.

But now Whitney claimed to have an important case for them. There was only one way to find out if she really did: go to the meeting.

"Do you think it's another phony case?" Corey asked Ben on their way to Whitney's locker.

"I guess we'll find out soon enough," Ben replied. "I can't exactly say that I trust Whitney and Alyssa after what they did. We should pay attention to their body language, to see if they give any signs that they're not being completely honest again."

"Good idea," Corey agreed. "I'll focus on Whitney and you keep an eye on Alyssa. And Hannah—"

"I don't think we need to worry about Hannah," Ben said with a grin. "She's onto both of them!"

When Ben and Corey arrived at Whitney's locker, Hannah, Alyssa, and Whitney were waiting for them. Whitney got right down to business. "So we have another case for you," she began. "And this one is for real."

"Go on," Hannah said.

Whitney glanced around to make sure no one

was listening. "This is top secret, okay," she said, lowering her voice. "Do you *swear* you won't repeat what I'm about to tell you?"

Club CSI exchanged glances, then nodded.

"Last night, I got into huge trouble," Whitney continued. "With my parents. I mean, seriously, seriously busted. But here's the thing . . . I didn't do anything wrong!"

"She didn't," Alyssa chimed in.

"Then why did you get in trouble?" asked Ben.

"Have you ever played that online drawing game?" Whitney asked. "You know the one. It's called You Can Draw It!"

Hannah and Corey nodded, but Ben shook his head. Hannah tried to explain. "It's this Internet game that's really big right now," she told him. "Basically, the game gives you a word, and you have to draw it by using your mouse and arrow keys. Then another player tries to guess what you're drawing. The more you play, the more points you earn, which you can use to get upgrades so that your pictures will look better."

"The upgrades are tools like extra colors or pattern packs or special features like sparkles or animation effects," Corey chimed in. "You definitely need a lot of upgrades to draw the best pictures."

Everyone turned to look at him.

"What?" he asked with a shrug. "I've played it a few times. It's pretty cool."

"But it takes a long time to earn enough points to get even one expansion pack," Whitney said. "So earning points isn't the only way you can get upgrades. You can also buy them for, like, ten dollars each; nine dollars and ninety-nine cents to be exact. And someone hacked into my account and bought ten expansion packs!"

Everyone immediately glanced over at Alyssa.

"Don't look at me," Alyssa said, holding up her hands. "First, I would never do something like that. It's totally stealing. Second, Whitney and I promised each other that we wouldn't go into each other's accounts. Not after what happened. We even changed the passwords on all of our accounts. We learned the hard way what can happen when you don't keep your password secret, even from your best friend."

As she spoke, Alyssa looked directly into Ben's eyes, then Corey's, and finally Hannah's.

"And third, I've never even played You Can Draw It!" Alyssa continued. "Drawing isn't my thing, you know?"

"So my parents got their credit card bill yesterday, and there was a charge for almost a hundred dollars from You Can Draw It!" Whitney continued. "They think *I* made that purchase—but I didn't!"

"Did you tell them that?" asked Corey.

"Of course I did," replied Whitney. "But they don't believe me. See, there was this one time—ugh, this is so embarrassing—I bought a shirt online and didn't tell them about it, so they think I did the same thing with the upgrades. And I was supposed to have this awesome party next Friday night, but my parents have grounded me for a month! I really, really, *really* don't want to cancel my party—I would, like, die. Everybody already knows about it!"

As Whitney talked, her voice got higher and higher. Alyssa put her arm around her friend to calm her down. "Hey, don't get upset," Alyssa said soothingly. "Club CSI will figure out who made those charges, and then you'll prove to your parents it wasn't you and you can still have your party. Everything's gonna be okay."

Whitney was too upset to be consoled. She shrugged off Alyssa's arm.

"No, it's not!" she cried. "Somebody is messing with me online, and I have no idea who it is—or how to stop them! Do they have all my passwords? What are they going to hack next? My e-mail? My IMs? Are they spying on my MyWorld profile? Are they reading my texts? What if they start forwarding stuff from my accounts to, like, everybody in school? It's, like, it's this huge, like—this awful—"

"Violation," Ben finished. "It's a violation of your online privacy."

"Yes," Whitney said, looking at him with relief. "That's what I was trying to say."

"So here's what we're gonna do," Corey spoke up. "Club CSI is going to talk this one over and let you know if we can help."

"I'll text you in a bit," Hannah promised. "And don't worry—We won't tell *anyone* what you've told us."

"And, you know, you shouldn't tell anyone else, either," Ben added. "Let's keep it between the five of us."

"Okay," Whitney said. She tried to smile. "Thanks."

There were still a few minutes until homeroom, so Corey, Ben, and Hannah hurried off to Club CSI's unofficial headquarters, a little-used hallway behind the gym. It was the one place in the whole school where they knew they could talk without being interrupted . . . or overheard.

"Well," Hannah said. "What do you think? Were Whitney and Alyssa telling the truth?"

"It's hard to say for sure," Ben replied. "I definitely think Alyssa is telling the truth—especially when you compare her body language to when we interviewed her about the e-mail."

"I agree," Hannah said. "And I kind of think that Whitney's telling the truth too."

"Really?" Ben asked. "Are you sure this isn't just another plot to spend time with Corey?"

"Yeah, I mean, who can resist?" Corey cracked.

"That isn't what's going on this time," Hannah replied, rolling her eyes. "No offense, Corey, but I think both Whitney and Alyssa have moved on. I heard Whitney is crushing on this guy on the baseball team. And Alyssa is going out with his best friend. Which is probably why they're both so desperate to keep Whitney's party from getting canceled."

"Oh. Yeah. Whatever," Corey replied, trying to act casual. "You know what they say. All's fair in love and baseball."

"So assuming Whitney didn't make those charges, this could be a really interesting case," Ben said. "I think we should take it."

"So do I," Hannah agreed.

"Me too," said Corey.

"So it's unanimous," Ben announced. "Club CSI is on the case!"

Chapter 9

C lub CSI began their investigation that afternoon at Whitney's house, as soon as she was finished with cheerleading practice.

"Hi, Mom," Whitney called as she walked through her front door and plunked her backpack down on the chair nearest the door. Hannah, Ben, and Corey were right behind her.

"Hi, dear," answered her mother, emerging from the next room. When she laid eyes on Club CSI, she frowned. "Whitney, what did we talk about last night? You're grounded. No one is allowed to come over."

"But Hannah, Ben, Corey, and I are just working on a project for school," Whitney pleaded. "Can they please stay for a little while? We won't have any fun, I promise. We'll just do some work."

Mrs. Martino sighed. "Fine," she relented. "But as soon as dinner is ready, everyone has to go home."

"Thanks, Mom!" Whitney said brightly as she breezed past her. Hannah, Ben, and Corey each mumbled hi to Mrs. Martino as they hurried to follow Whitney.

"So, here's my laptop," Whitney said when they entered the den. "Do your detective stuff and tell me who hacked my account."

"If only it were that easy," Ben said. "Let's talk for a little while first."

Whitney shrugged. "Sure. Whatever you want."

"Tell us about your experience with You Can Draw It!" Corey began as he flopped on to a large beanbag chair. "When did you sign up for an account?"

"I don't remember exactly," Whitney admitted. "Maybe three weeks ago? I was bored one night so I thought I'd check it out. But when I played it, I just didn't get into it. It seemed like a ton of work to earn enough points for the upgrades, and without the upgrades, all my pictures looked like garbage. So I logged out and kind of forgot I'd even signed up . . . until my parents got that bill."

"So you used their credit card when you signed up?" asked Ben.

"Yeah. You don't have to put credit card info in when you sign up, but I did," Whitney replied. "That was before I knew how much the upgrades cost. I would have asked my parents before I bought any."

"And did you ever buy any?" Corey asked. "Even just one, to see what it was like?"

"For ten dollars? No way," Whitney said, shaking her head. "I'd rather get some nail polish or new earrings or something like that."

"When you signed up for the game, did you also sign up for the e-mail notifications they send?" Hannah asked.

"No, I get enough spam already," Whitney replied. "I only got one e-mail from the game, ever, and that was right after I signed up. It had my username and password in it, but I never showed it to anybody."

"Can I take a look at your computer?" Ben asked.

"Go ahead," Whitney said. "Here, I'll log on to the Internet for you."

"Thanks," Ben said. "Let's check the browser history to see which websites have been accessed from this computer."

With a few quick keystrokes, Ben was able to access a list of every website that had been visited from Whitney's computer in the last month. He scrolled through a long list of the same sites—Whitney's e-mail provider, her MyWorld account, the cheerleading squad's message board, and a few fashion blogs. Then, dated exactly three weeks ago, he found it—one visit to the You Can Draw It! website.

Club CSI didn't need to talk about it to know that the browser confirmed Whitney's story: She hadn't played You Can Draw It! on her laptop since the first time she signed up.

"I can't believe my laptop keeps a record of every single site I've been to," Whitney said as she stared at the screen, and then she looked at Ben. "It's cool that you know so much about them."

"Yeah, computers know a lot," Corey joked. "Almost as much as Ben."

"If you say so," Ben replied. Then he keyed in a new web address. "Let's check out your You Can Draw It! account. Whitney, can you log in for me?"

Whitney leaned across the desk to type in her username and password.

"Huh. This game does look kind of interesting," Ben said thoughtfully as he scrolled through the website. "Maybe I should sign up for an account too. Or maybe not, if they're easy to hack. Anyway, let's see what's been going on with Whitney's account."

Ben clicked on the Account Settings tab. When the page loaded, he let out a low whistle. "Well, Whitney, you might not have been using your account—but someone else has," he said. "According to your account's usage history, you've logged on to your account ten times since you signed up!"

Whitney's mouth dropped open. "Are you kidding me?" she exclaimed.

But Ben wasn't joking. The proof was on the screen in front of them. And every time the hacker had logged on, they had purchased an upgrade pack.

"Also, look at this," Ben said. "There's a pattern here. The hacker always played sometime after five p.m. and before seven p.m."

"Then it *definitely* wasn't me, because I'm nowhere near a computer around dinnertime," Whitney said. "My mom is really strict about family dinner. It's always at five thirty. Every day. Nobody's allowed to use computers or cell phones or anything—not even my dad. And I have to clean up, so I'm not free again till around seven."

"Wait. Back on the main page, Whitney's drawing tools didn't have any upgrades," Hannah realized. "So where are the expansion packs?"

Ben clicked another tab. "Here you go," he said. "They were immediately gifted to three different players—jojo2020, LOL1234, and Dancer99." Ben glanced at Whitney. "Do any of those usernames sound familiar?"

"No," Whitney answered. "I've never chatted or e-mailed with any of those players."

"So if you haven't been playing from your computer at home and you were having dinner with your family when the charges were made, there's no way that you did it," Hannah said. "I think we have enough evidence to prove to your parents you're innocent."

"Mom! Dad!" Whitney yelled at the top her voice. "Can you come into the den?"

A few moments later, Mr. Martino strolled into the room. Mrs. Martino followed him, wiping her hands on a dish towel.

"Whitney, I have asked you not to yell—Oh

hello," Mr. Martino said when he saw Club CSI.

"This is Corey, Ben, and Hannah," Whitney told her parents. "They have this club that solves mysteries, and they can *prove* I didn't put any charges on your credit card!"

Mrs. Martino sighed. "Whitney. We've already been through this. Your father and I are not going to—"

"Please, just listen to what they have to say," Whitney begged.

"We'll be quick, promise," Corey said, flashing her a smile.

Mr. Martino shrugged. "Go ahead, then."

Ben showed Whitney's parents the browser history on her laptop, then explained how the account history proved that someone else had been playing the game.

Mr. Martino put on his reading glasses and squinted at the screen. "Hmm. I didn't realize that," he said.

"Well, I *told* you," Whitney said, pouting.

"Well, then, I'm doubly glad we unlinked our credit card from this game. Now this hacker person won't be able to run up any more charges,"

Mr. Martino said as he sat down at the computer.

"I'm sorry, Whitney," said Mrs. Martino as she gave her daughter a hug. "We'll open a dispute with the credit card company. You're not grounded anymore."

"So I can have my party?" Whitney said hopefully.

Mrs. Martino smiled at her. "Yes, of course you can."

"Yes! Yes! Yes!" Whitney shrieked. She dove across her dad and started sending an instant message. "I have to tell Alyssa right away so we can start planning again. We are *so* behind. We lost, like, an entire day!"

Ben cleared his throat. "Um, Whitney," he began. "It's great that you're not grounded anymore, but the case is still open. We want to find out *who* hacked your account. After all, this hacker could strike someone else's account, and we should find them before that happens. So you and Alyssa shouldn't tell anyone about the hacking or the charges, okay?"

"Sure, whatever," Whitney said with her eyes glued to the screen. "I think I'll just delete my You Can Draw It! account since I'm never going to play it again, anyway."

"Actually, could you keep your account for a few more days?" Hannah spoke up. "Just until we finish investigating?"

Whitney glanced at her parents.

"I guess that's okay," Mrs. Martino said slowly, "since the credit card isn't linked anymore."

"You should change the passwords on all your other accounts, though," Ben suggested. "Just to be on the safe side."

"That's good advice," Mr. Martino said. "Whitney, I want you to start changing *all* your passwords every month."

"Cool. Whatever," Whitney said as she chatted online with Alyssa.

"You're certainly welcome to stay for dinner," Mrs. Martino told Club CSI.

At the mention of food, Corey's eyes lit up, but he knew he had to be home for dinner tonight. "Thanks, Mrs. Martino, but we'd better get going," Corey replied. "Bye, Whitney."

"Bye," she replied, still staring at the screen. Then she turned around in her chair. "And thanks, you guys. I really owe you."

"No problem," Corey said. "That's what Club CSI

is here for. We'll keep you posted on the rest of our investigation."

As the three friends walked toward home, they talked about the case.

"So what are we going to do next?" Corey asked. "Our only witness is the hacker. We don't even have any suspects."

"Sure we do," Hannah said. "Alyssa, for one."

"But we all agreed she was telling the truth this morning," Corey pointed out.

"True," Hannah said. "But we know for a fact that she went into one of Whitney's accounts before. So even if she's at the bottom of the list, she still belongs there."

"Hannah's right," Ben chimed in. "Is there anyone else at school who might hack into Whitney's account? Or want to get her in trouble?"

"What about Whitney's party?" Corey asked suddenly. "What if somebody who didn't get invited wanted revenge? Maybe they wanted the whole party to get canceled."

"That's possible," Hannah said thoughtfully. "And if that's what's going on, the hacker might strike again." She was quiet for a moment. "You know what? Maybe Whitney's ex-friend Maya should be on the list."

"But wasn't their fight a long time ago?" Ben asked.

"It was last year," Hannah replied. "But even if Maya is over the fight, she must know about the party. It's *the* eighth-grade event. Maybe she's mad Whitney didn't invite her."

"We should definitely interview Maya, then," Corey said right away.

Hannah smiled at him. "*You* should," she teased.

"What we really need to do is figure out who jojo2020, LOL1234, and Dancer99 are," Ben said. "Those players are as close to witnesses as we're going to get."

"But everybody who plays You Can Draw It! is anonymous," Hannah pointed out. "That's the whole point of having usernames."

"I know," Ben replied. "That's what makes this case so tough."

"So we're just going to have to step up our game, then," Corey said confidently. He faked like he was dunking a basketball. "Slam dunk! Game over! Case closed!"

Chapter 10

Club CSI met for breakfast the next morning at the school cafeteria to go over some new developments.

"So I tried to get in touch with Zazzam last night," Ben began.

"Za-what?" Corey asked.

"Zazzam," repeated Ben. "That's the company that owns You Can Draw It! So I tried to get in touch with them. Believe me, it's not easy. It's like they don't want people contacting them."

"Maybe they get a lot of complaints that their games are too hard," Corey suggested. "Or that the expansion packs cost too much."

"Maybe," Ben said. "I had to do a lot of digging, but I finally found an e-mail address, so I sent an e-mail asking if they could give me more information about some You Can Draw It! players. There was a response in my in-box this morning."

"And?" Corey asked hopefully.

"And nothing," Ben replied. He shook his head. "They wouldn't give me anything, not even the e-mail addresses those players used when they signed up. They said it was confidential information, and it's part of the user agreement that they wouldn't release it."

"It stinks that they wouldn't even give you the e-mail addresses," Hannah said.

"Yeah," Ben said. "I guess that's a dead end."

"Well, I e-mailed Maya last night," Corey said. "She agreed to meet us before homeroom, so she should be here any second."

"Oh good," Hannah said. "Do you know what you're going to say during the interview?"

"I have it all planned out," Corey said. "I'm going for the kind, gentle Corey. Poor Maya's been through enough—losing her best friends, having her heart broken, becoming a total pariah . . ."

Hannah frowned. "Well, it wasn't *quite* that dramatic—"

"I'm just saying, she could probably use a little friendship right now," Corey continued. "And then maybe she'll tell her new friends about what she did. The weight of a guilty conscience is a heavy burden to bear."

"Oh yeah?" Hannah asked. "Then where is she? The bell is gonna ring in less than five minutes."

A flicker of doubt crossed Corey's face. "I don't know," he admitted. "She *said* she'd be here."

Club CSI waited in the cafeteria until the second bell, just in case Maya was late. Then they had to run to make it to homeroom before being marked late themselves. And by that time, it was very clear that Maya had stood them up.

• ◦ • ◗ ◖ ▔• ◗ •

Corey was still fuming at lunchtime. "I can't believe she just didn't show up!" he complained to Ben and Hannah as they waited in line. "I can show you guys our e-mail exchange. I very clearly asked her to meet us in the cafeteria before homeroom, and she very clearly said yes! You know what? Maybe she *is* guilty. Maybe *she's* the one who hacked Whitney's account! Maybe we're getting too close and that's why Maya never showed! She's avoiding us!"

"Or not," Hannah said. "She's sitting right there."

Corey blinked. "Oh. She is? Well, the interview starts *now*, then. Or right after I pay for this delicious—What is this we're eating today?"

"Empanadas," Ben said helpfully. "They're like pastries filled with spicy beef. They smell delicious."

"There are some with vegetables," Hannah added. "And some with black beans and cheese, too."

"Awesome. I want three of each," Corey said.

Corey filled his tray, paid for his meal, and walked straight over to Maya's table. "Hey, Maya," he said. "It's Corey. Good to see you. What happened? You're, like, five hours late."

Maya's shoulders hunched as she crossed her arms in front of her. "Oh yeah, that was today. I forgot."

Corey didn't need to analyze Maya's body language to tell she was lying, but he wasn't going to let that get in his way. "No worries. We can talk now. What do you say—your table or mine?"

Maya sighed and rolled her eyes. "Be right back, Rachel," she told her friend. "I don't want to bore you with this." Then she picked up her tray and followed Corey over to Club CSI's usual table, where Ben and Hannah were waiting.

Corey sat down across from Maya, took a huge bite of his lunch, and immediately started to feel better—not only because the empanadas were just as delicious as they smelled, but because as he looked at the scowl on Maya's face, he knew he'd have to use his best interview skills to find out if Maya really was a suspect.

And Corey was ready for the challenge.

"So what's going on, Maya?" he asked in a friendly voice.

"You tell me," Maya said flatly. She had crossed her arms again. "You're the one who e-mailed me."

"Yeah, thanks for talking to us," Corey said. He paused to see if Maya would apologize for skipping their earlier meeting. When she didn't, he wondered if Maya's attitude was actually a sign of her guilt.

Then Corey remembered something Miss Hodges had said: Just because someone lies during an interview, it doesn't mean they're guilty. He guessed the same thing could be said of a bad attitude.

"So, the three of us—Hannah and Ben and I—have this club," Corey continued. "It's called Club

CSI, and we investigate crimes that happen at Woodlands."

"Or to students," added Hannah.

"And this has what to do with me?" Maya asked.

"Someone you know had one of her online accounts hacked," Corey explained. "So we're trying to find out more by interviewing her friends—and, uh, former friends."

Ben shot Corey a look across the table. He hadn't planned to bring up Whitney so early in the interview. But it was too late; Maya knew exactly who Corey meant. She exhaled loudly in frustration.

"Are you even kidding me?" Maya exclaimed. "Did Whitney tell you I did it? Did she say it was me? I swear, I am so *sick* of her—"

"Whoa, no way, not at all," Corey interrupted her. "We're just talking to everyone who knows her."

Maya sighed and looked at the table. When she looked up again, she seemed calmer. "Sorry. It's just—Whitney and I haven't been friends in a long time. But everybody's still talking about the fight we had. It's so dumb."

"No kidding," Corey said sympathetically. "You just wish people would forget about it already."

"Exactly!" Maya exclaimed. Then she actually gave Corey a small smile.

"What do you think people don't know about the fight?" Corey asked. "What do you wish you could tell everybody?"

Maya's forehead furrowed as she thought about Corey's questions. "That the past is the past, and that's where it should stay—in the past," she replied. "That I've moved on, and everybody else should too."

"You don't miss being friends with Whitney and Alyssa?" Hannah asked.

"Not really," Maya told her. "I have new friends now, and I'm really tight with them. The people in drama, for example. That's why I quit cheerleading. I actually like acting a lot more."

"So if Whitney invited you to a party, would you go?" Ben said.

Maya's laugh was short. "Oh, is that what this is about?" she asked. "I heard about her big party, and you know what? I seriously don't even care. I mean, I wouldn't go if Whitney got down on her knees and begged me. You know why?"

"Why?" said Corey.

"Because my new best friend, Rachel, got us tickets to see Jasmine Ayle in concert that night! The concert is sold out!" A huge grin spread across Maya's face. "You can go ask Rachel if you want. Honestly, I hope Whitney's party is awesome. Because I'm pretty sure seeing Jasmine Ayle *live* will be even more awesome!"

"Of course," Corey said, grinning back. He exchanged a look with Ben, and he knew he wasn't the only one at the table who didn't have a clue who Jasmine Ayle was. "You'll have a great time! Thanks for talking to us about the case."

"No problem," Maya replied. "See you around, guys."

Hannah, Corey, and Ben watched Maya return to her table and sit next to Rachel. They started chatting and laughing together right away. Even from across the cafeteria, Club CSI could tell that Maya and Rachel were really good friends.

Corey spoke first. "I'm not feeling it, guys," he said. "I don't think she's the hacker."

"Neither do I," Ben said as Hannah nodded. "At first, I wasn't sure. She seemed so defensive and almost angry."

"The way she was acting did seem kind of suspicious," Hannah spoke up. "Like she was hiding something—and mad at us for trying to figure out what it was."

"Exactly!" Ben said. "But it really seems like she's tired of talking about the fight. I can't say I blame her."

"Me neither," Hannah said.

"So Alyssa . . . Is she still at the bottom of our list?" Corey said.

"Yeah," Ben said. "Why? Do you have a feeling or something?"

"Not really," Corey said. "It's just that she's pretty much the *only* possible suspect we have."

"Do you think another interview would help?" Hannah asked.

"I guess." Corey shrugged. "But Whitney already told Alyssa everything. We're going to need some new info before we can question her."

"I agree," Ben said. "And I've been thinking it's time to take our investigation to the next level."

"What do you mean?" Corey said.

"I think it's time to go inside the game," Ben replied.

Chapter 11

Hannah and Corey went over to Ben's house after school. They wanted to continue their investigation right away, but decided to tackle their homework first (after Corey's snack), especially since Ben had a feeling that the next stage of their investigation might take a little while.

"Done!" Corey announced when he finished checking over his math homework. "So what's next?"

"Here's what I'm thinking," Ben began. "We keep talking about how this crime has no witnesses, which makes it harder to find suspects. But we're wrong. There *are* witnesses."

"Who?" Corey and Hannah asked at the same time.

"Jojo20, LOL1234, and Dancer99!" Ben announced.

"They're the ones who received the stolen expansion packs, after all. So they have to know something."

"And who knows?" Hannah said. "Maybe one of them is the hacker!"

"Maybe," Ben said. "Now, I wasn't able to get any information on them from Zazzam last night. Then, during gym today, I had an idea: If we start playing You Can Draw It!, we can make contact with them through the game itself!"

"That's a great idea!" exclaimed Hannah. Then her face fell. "But, um, I don't want to use my account. If that's okay."

"Me neither," Corey added.

"No, of course not," Ben said. He logged on to the Internet and went to the You Can Draw It! website. "We should definitely open a new account for this."

Ben was quiet for a moment as he set up an account without putting in any credit card information (of course). Then he looked up at Hannah and Corey. "How does this username sound to you?"

"HBCCSI," Hannah read. "Let me guess: Hannah, Ben, Corey, CSI. Sounds good to me."

"Ben! Dinnertime!" Ben's mom called from the kitchen.

"That always happens to me, too! Just when I'm about to get on the computer, it's time to eat," Corey said. "Not that I'm complaining or anything. Whatever your mom cooked smells *good*."

"Don't worry," Ben said. "I just looked up jojo2020, LOL1234, and Dancer99. They're not online right now. But remember what we learned at Whitney's last night?"

"The thief usually plays in the evening," Corey replied.

"And if the thief knows jojo2020, LOL1234, and Dancer99, maybe they'll be playing in the evening too," Ben replied. "Come on, let's go eat—and when we get back to the computer, maybe one of our mystery players will be online."

By the time dinner was over, it was almost dark outside. The only light in Ben's room was a creepy blue glow from the computer monitor, which cast strange shadows around his room. Ben flipped a switch, flooding the room with light—but Hannah still felt a little uneasy.

"Do you think . . . maybe this isn't a good idea?"

she asked the boys. "I mean, we don't have any idea who these mystery players are. It just seems a little . . . I don't know . . ."

"Weird?" Corey volunteered.

"Yeah," Hannah said. "Or scary. I mean, maybe they're just kids who go to our school. Or maybe they're part of some giant international computer-hacking crime ring!"

"With names like LOL and Dancer?" Corey asked, cracking a smile.

"Actually, Corey, Hannah's right," Ben said thoughtfully. "That's the thing about connecting with strangers online—you really don't know who's on the other end, even if they have a username that sounds like something your friend would have. It could be . . . anybody, really. Anybody in the world."

He clicked over to HBCCSI's profile. "Hannah, check this out," Ben continued. "I set our profile to private and made sure that the e-mail address we signed up with is hidden. And our real names and ages aren't connected to the account at all. There's no way for other users to contact us—or even learn anything about us."

"Okay," Hannah said. "That makes me feel better, I guess."

"Should I ask jojo2020, LOL1234, and Dancer99 to be friends with us?" he asked, sliding into a chair.

"Yeah, go ahead," Ben said.

Corey sent the game's automated friend message to each name. Suddenly, each player's name appeared in a list at the side of the screen.

Ping!

Ping!

Ping!

All three players approved HBCCSI instantly!

"Now we're in business!" Corey exclaimed. "Should I challenge them to a draw-off?"

"That might take a while," Hannah said. "Let's just jump right in and send them a message."

She leaned across Corey and double-clicked jojo2020's username.

"What are you going to say?" asked Ben.

Hannah started typing in the message box. "How does this look?" she asked.

can you tell me how to get free upgrade packs? don't want to pay.

"I like it," Ben replied. "It's straight, direct . . ."

"And definitely to the point," Corey added. "Let's send the same message to LOL1234 and Dancer99, too."

Hannah copied the text and pasted it into two more chat windows. "Done . . . and done," she said. "Corey, you want to send them?"

It only took three clicks of the mouse. Then the instant messages were winging their way through cyberspace. Club CSI didn't speak as they stared at the three instant-message windows. There was a green light blinking next to each mystery player's username.

"So now we wait for a response," Ben said, breaking the silence.

They didn't have to wait long.

Almost immediately, the green lights went out: first LOL1234, then jojo2020, then Dancer99. A message popped up in each chat window: USER IS NO LONGER ONLINE.

Hannah raised her eyebrows. "I guess they're not interested in chatting," she noted.

Corey clicked over to HBCCSI's friends list. All three names had disappeared there, too. "No friends? I've never felt so unpopular in my whole life!" he joked.

"Try a search for their usernames," Ben suggested.

Corey typed 'jojo2020' into the Find Players box. A message from the game flashed on to the screen.

There is no user by this name.

"That's not right," Corey said. "Hello, we just messaged jojo2020."

"Maybe jojo2020 deleted their account!" Hannah exclaimed. "Quick, try LOL1234."

Corey tried another search—and got the same message.

"Now try Dancer99," Ben said.

Once again, a window from the game popped up. But this time the message was different.

This user's profile is private.

"So jojo2020 and LOL1234 deleted their accounts," Ben said. "But Dancer99 didn't. Try sending another message."

Corey double-clicked Dancer99's username—and got a big surprise.

This user has blocked incoming messages from you.

Hannah, Ben, and Corey looked at one another. Their eyes were wide.

"I think we have a suspect," Ben said.

"Which one?" Hannah asked.

"All of them!" Corey replied. "What if jojo2020, LOL1234, and Dancer99 are all the same person? Maybe this person just got our message three times."

"That would make sense," Hannah said slowly. "Dancer99—let's say that's the hacker's main account—breaks into Whitney's account and buys ten upgrades. But she doesn't just gift them to herself—that's too obvious, right? So she creates a couple of fake accounts that can then gift the upgrades back to the main account—Dancer99."

"'She'?" Ben repeated.

Hannah shrugged. "Just a guess. The username

'dancer' could be a guy, but it's more likely a girl, right?"

"Good point," Ben replied. "But if this was some kind of misdirection strategy, it seems like a *lot* of work just to score a few upgrades for a computer game, though."

"And how could we ever prove it?" Corey added.

"Let's tackle one question at a time," Hannah proposed. "Maybe if we can answer Ben's question, we'll figure out how to find the answer to Corey's."

"Hey, Corey, can I have a turn?" Ben asked. "I've never played You Can Draw It! before."

"Sure, go ahead," Corey replied as he slid out of the chair. Then he showed Ben how to start a new game with another anonymous player.

"You can type in a player's username," Corey explained. "Or you can click 'Random Challenge,' and the game will pick a player for you."

Just then Ben noticed a small box in the top right corner of the screen. A long number in it changed with every passing second. "There are 709,112 people playing? Right now?" he asked.

"I know," Corey said. "This game is really popular. Especially now, in the evening—probably because kids have just finished their homework and they're logging on to play for a while before going to bed."

"What's that?" Ben asked, pointing at a sparkling gold star in the corner of the screen. When he moved the cursor over the star, the words "WIN BIG!" flashed in rainbow colors.

"Click it," Hannah suggested.

A new page loaded immediately.

YOU CAN DRAW IT!
FIRST ANNUAL DRAWATHON
DRAW TILL YOU DROP!
Do you have what it takes to be the next great artist? Here at the You Can Draw It! headquarters, we've been looking at your artwork . . . and we like what we see. In fact, we like it so much that we're willing to pay BIG MONEY to the best picture submitted by May 1. Twenty-five finalists will be selected for a featured page in the Gallery, where other You Can Draw It! users will vote on their favorite picture. The artist whose picture gets the most votes wins eternal fame, glory, and . . . $2,500!

"Twenty-five hundred dollars!" Hannah exclaimed. "That's a ton of money! What a great prize."

"No kidding," Ben said. "It's also a great motive. Didn't you say the upgrade packs help players make better pictures?"

"Definitely," Corey said.

"So someone who really, really wanted to win this contest might think she wouldn't stand a chance without a bunch of upgrades," said Hannah.

"And if she couldn't afford them . . . ," Ben said.

He didn't need to finish his sentence.

Club CSI knew exactly what he meant.

"What's this Gallery thing?" Ben asked as he clicked the link, which led him to a slow-loading page.

"Oh, when you finish a picture, you can upload it to the Gallery," Hannah replied as one by one, hundreds of thumbnail images began to load. "Other players can look at pictures here for inspiration, and you can vote on the ones you like the best. You can even search for pictures from specific users."

Ben immediately typed "Dancer99" into the search field. Seven pictures appeared on the screen, including a meadow filled with purple flowers and a princess wearing a fancy gown with ribbon trim.

Corey whistled. "Her pictures are awesome. It must have taken hours to do that princess one," he said.

"Look at all the textures in the dress," Hannah said. "She definitely used an upgrade to draw that."

"So here's our theory," Ben began. "Dancer99 wants to win the grand prize, but needs expansion packs to do it. So she hacks Whitney's account, buys ten upgrades on Mrs. Martino's credit card, and gives them to fake accounts as a decoy. Then the fake accounts transfer the upgrades back to Dancer99, who uses them to make pictures like that princess one."

"It's a good theory," Corey said. "Now all we have to do is prove it. . . . But how?"

Club CSI sat quietly for a few minutes, everyone lost in thought.

"You know what I think?" Hannah finally said. "I think it's time to talk to Miss Hodges."

Chapter 12

Much to the dismay of Corey's growling stomach, instead of rushing right to the cafeteria after forensic science the next day, Club CSI hung around to talk to Miss Hodges.

"Ah, my favorite club," Miss Hodges said cheerfully. "What can I do for you?"

Hannah, Ben, and Corey scanned the room just to make sure they were the only students inside. After all, Dancer99 could be anyone.

"We have a new case," Ben explained. "But we've kind of hit a wall and don't know what to try next."

Miss Hodges put down her pen. "Tell me what you've got."

Club CSI recapped their investigation into the hacking of Whitney's You Can Draw It! account.

"So our theory is that Dancer99 hacked the account and bought the upgrades . . . but we're not sure how to prove it," Ben finished.

"And even though Whitney's parents have opened a fraud claim with the credit card company, and won't be responsible for the charges, we still want to find out *who* did it," Hannah added. "If we can, I mean."

"Of course you do," Miss Hodges said. "I want to know too! Your investigation falls under an exciting branch of forensic science called digital forensics."

"Really? It has its own field and everything?" asked Corey.

"Yes. Unfortunately, there're plenty of crimes in cyberspace," Miss Hodges said. "Account hacking, identity theft, unauthorized credit card usage, stolen personal information, digital espionage. Everyone from individual citizens to major corporations to governments around the globe must be aware of the threat that cyber criminals pose. And the best ones often leave no trail, making them even harder to track. But that doesn't sound like what you've already discovered about this Dancer99."

Miss Hodges paused as she reached into her bag

for her cell phone. "I don't know enough about digital forensics to help you figure out your next steps, but my friend Mitch Carlton might," she continued. "He's a web developer and an online gaming expert. Are you free after school today? I'll text Mitch to see if he can come by and advise you."

"Yes, absolutely!" Ben replied right away.

Club CSI waited quietly while Miss Hodges sent the text to Mr. Carlton. "We should hear back from him pretty quickly," Miss Hodges said. "He's basically online twenty-four hours a—"

Bzzzz! Miss Hodges grinned. "Right on time!" she said. Then she read the text aloud. "'Sounds interesting. I'll be there at three o'clock. MC.'"

"Cool!" Corey cheered. "So should we meet you here after school?"

"I'll have to sign Mitch in at the office," Miss Hodges said. "So let's meet at the computer lab instead. See you after school!"

"Thanks, Miss Hodges," said Ben, and then he turned around to walk to the cafeteria with Hannah and Corey. But only Hannah was there.

"I guess Corey couldn't wait any longer for lunch," Hannah said with a smile.

After school, Club CSI staked out a computer in the back corner of the lab. When Miss Hodges appeared in the doorway, Hannah waved to catch her attention. Miss Hodges was followed by a man whose black hair was slicked back into a short ponytail. He wore a large badge around his neck that read WOODLANDS JUNIOR HIGH SCHOOL: VISITOR.

"Oh, here they are," Miss Hodges said to Mr. Carlton. "Mitch, this is Ben, Corey, and Hannah, the founding members of Club CSI. Everyone, this is Mr. Carlton."

"Hey, Club CSI," Mr. Carlton said. He pulled a chair over to the computer station and turned it around so that he was sitting on it backward. "Miss Hodges told me so many great things about you guys and your club. It's nice to meet you!"

"I told Mr. Carlton everything about the case, so he's completely up to speed," Miss Hodges continued as she rolled another chair over to their computer station. "Take it away!"

"Our big challenge right now is figuring out who is the person behind a particular username, Mr.

Carlton," Ben said. "We're pretty sure that Dancer99 is the one who purchased the expansion packs. But unless we can find out who Dancer99 really is, we've reached a dead end."

"Is that something you know how to do?" Corey asked hopefully. "Find out the real identity behind an online one?"

Mr. Carlton shook his head. "Look, sometimes it *can* be done," he replied. "Especially by law officers after a crime has been committed—but even they need a court order. But for civilians like us, that kind of hacking would just result in more laws being broken—if we could even get through the security protections on a game like You Can Draw It!"

"What do you mean by that—'security protections'?" Hannah asked.

"Commercial websites for gaming companies, or shopping sites, use complicated codes to encrypt their users' personal information," Mr. Carlton explained. "If a site is hacked and that information is stolen, people will be less likely to visit the site. So, these companies spend a lot of time and money doing everything they can to prevent hacking."

"So that makes it more likely that whoever

hacked Whitney's account already knew her password," Ben said.

Mr. Carlton nodded. "When a professional hacker breaks into a site, they will steal tons of data," he said. "Thousands of users' personal information, credit card numbers, passwords—that sort of thing. Then the hacker can sell it to other criminals. So it usually becomes a big news story, and at the very least, the company that was hacked will send an e-mail to its users urging them to change their passwords and monitor their accounts. And I haven't heard of any wide-scale hacking of You Can Draw It!"

"Mr. Carlton would know," Miss Hodges spoke up. "He's one of the moderators on Hacker Tracker, a blog and message board that reports Internet crimes."

"Okay . . . ," Hannah said slowly. "If there's no way to figure out *who* Dancer99 really is, what next? Is this the end of our investigation? Because I don't really think we can get court orders or anything."

Mr. Carlton tapped his fingers on the desk as he thought about it. "There might be one other option," he finally said. "You know *when* Dancer99 was logging on to Whitney's account, right?"

"Yeah," Corey said.

"So maybe we can find out *where* Dancer99 was logging on," Mr. Carlton said. "You see, each computer has a unique identifier called an—"

"IP address!" Club CSI exclaimed all at once. Everyone laughed. Mr. Carlton looked impressed.

"Told you they were smart," Miss Hodges said proudly.

"So you can do that?" Ben asked Mr. Carlton. "You can find the IP addresses for where a game was played? I knew you could do it for e-mails, sometimes—but not for game play."

"Let's log on and see," Mr. Carlton suggested. "Except we do need to log on to Whitney's account. Will she give us permission to do that?"

"Let me text her," Hannah said as she reached for her cell phone. "Hopefully we can reach her before cheerleading practice starts. I know that Regionals is tomorrow."

Hannah's phone beeped almost immediately, and Hannah looked up from her phone with a big smile. "Whitney's cool with us accessing her account, and she just sent her log-on info, too."

Hannah typed Whitney's username and password

into the You Can Draw It! sign-in screen. Then she turned to Mr. Carlton. "Where will we find the IP addresses of her last log-ons?"

"Click on Account Settings," Mr. Carlton instructed. "Then User Controls. Then Privacy. Okay, click the little box next to 'Allow me to access account history.' Good. Now go back to Account Settings."

"Look," Ben said, pointing at the screen. "There's a new option there: History."

"Exactly!" Mr. Carlton replied.

"That was kind of complicated to find," Corey said. "How did you even know about it?"

Mr. Carlton smiled. "One of my friends helped design You Can Draw It!," he explained. "I know he likes to embed lots of special features into the user controls—in case anyone needs it. So I shot him an e-mail after Miss Hodges texted me and he explained how to do this."

"Wow! That's really cool that you know the creator of You Can Draw It!" gushed Corey. "Is he judging the contest?"

"I don't know," said Mitch. "But I'm sure he'll have something to do with it. He feels really proud that his game is inspiring so much creativity."

"Go on, Hannah," Ben encouraged her. "Click History."

When Hannah did, a new screen popped up immediately. It included the date and time of every log-on . . . and the IP address for each one!

Ben frowned at the screen. "Log-on number one and log-on number twelve have the same IP address," he said. "That must be Whitney's laptop. "And log-on number thirteen is now—so that's the school computer's IP address. But the other ten IP addresses look really, really familiar."

"Well, yeah," Corey said. "They're practically the same, except for a couple digits."

"All those computers are on the same network, then," Mr. Carlton said. "Like in the computer lab here—each computer has a unique IP address, but they'll be very similar since they're connected to one network."

"No . . . ," Ben said slowly. "The similarity . . . It's more than that."

"Let's plot them on a map," Mr. Carlton suggested.

Hannah opened a new window and typed in the URL for the website that mapped IP addresses. Then she pasted in the IP address from the first hacking

of Whitney's account, which had happened at 5:09 p.m. on Wednesday, April 4.

"Twelve-fifty Oak Street!" she exclaimed. "That's the new branch of the library!"

"That's it!" Ben exclaimed. He dug around in his backpack and pulled out his evidence folder for the case. He showed everyone a crumpled piece of paper: the printout of the e-mail Alyssa sent to herself from Whitney's account. "That's why I recognized the IP address. . . . It's identical to the one where Alyssa hacked into Whitney's e-mail and sent that fake message."

"So the same computer was used for both crimes, on the same day . . . ," Corey began.

"Just thirteen minutes apart," Hannah realized as she checked the e-mail's time stamp. "So if Alyssa was using that computer to hack Whitney's e-mail . . . and then, thirteen minutes later, Dancer99 used the *same* computer to hack Whitney's You Can Draw It! account and charge the expansion packs . . ."

"Then it looks like we've found our suspect," Corey finished for her.

Chapter 13

On a beautiful springtime Saturday, school was the last place Club CSI wanted to be— but they didn't want to wait until Monday to interview Alyssa again. So they went up to the top of the bleachers during the Regionals cheerleading competition, watching cheerleaders from each school show off their best moves for the judges. Right now, Woodlands Junior High was up and Corey, Ben, and Hannah couldn't believe how athletic their cheerleading squad was, especially Whitney.

"Wow, did you *see* Whitney's back flip?" Hannah asked. "That was awesome! I never knew that she was so good at gymnastics."

"Yeah, Alyssa's pretty good too," added Corey. "A

pretty good liar. It's hard to believe, especially when she came clean before about going into Whitney's e-mail."

"It *is* creepy to think she could look us straight in the eye and lie like that," Hannah said. She squinted in the bright sunlight.

"Hey, Alyssa's still only a suspect," Ben reminded his friends. "Innocent until proven guilty, right? I know the evidence looks bad, but there's still a possibility she didn't do it."

"Definitely," Corey agreed. "And maybe when she knows what we know—I mean, she knows it already, obviously, she was the one using that computer—but when she knows how much we know, then maybe she'll tell the truth. That's how it happened with the e-mail before. As soon as Alyssa realized what we had figured out—"

"She confessed everything," Hannah interrupted as the Woodlands team finished competing. "I think they're going to present trophies as soon as the judges tally the scores, but let's go hang out by the locker room. I don't want to miss Alyssa."

"Er . . . no, thanks," Corey said. "Everyone will think Ben and I are freak shows if we're lurking around the locker room after the cheerleading competition."

"Fine." Hannah sighed. *"I'll* go wait there and bring Alyssa back to the bleachers so we can all interview her."

It took more than half an hour for the trophies to be awarded—Woodlands Junior High took second place—but eventually Hannah returned to the bleachers with Alyssa . . . and Whitney. Ben raised his eyebrows. He hadn't expected to question Alyssa with Whitney around.

"I know," Hannah said right away. "But Whitney insisted. She said—"

"I said it's *my* case and *my* account, so whatever you have to say to Alyssa, you can say to me too," Whitney interrupted. "Now let's get on with it because we're missing out on the celebration."

Club CSI could tell from Whitney's tone of voice that she meant it. If they wanted to question Alyssa at all, they would have to do it in front of Whitney— like it or not.

Corey patted a spot on the bleacher next to him. "Want to sit?" he asked Alyssa. She looked at him suspiciously, then perched on the edge of the bench.

"So . . . you guys want to talk to me about something?" Alyssa said. She sounded a little nervous. "I already told you that I didn't go into Whitney's You Can Draw It! account. And I *definitely* didn't make those purchases."

"But somebody did," Corey replied. "And whoever hacked into Whitney's account did it from the same computer where you sent the fake e-mail . . . just a few minutes afterward."

"And I'm telling you *it wasn't me*," Alyssa said firmly. "I'll say it again and again and again. I don't care. I swear I'm telling the truth. I've *never* played You Can Draw It! in my whole life, and I definitely didn't log in using Whitney's account. I don't even know her username!"

"Okay," Hannah said. "We hear you. But how do you explain it that the game hacker just happened to be using the same computer at almost exactly the same time you were?"

Alyssa glared at Hannah. "I don't know. Lots of people use those computers. Besides, how do we even know you're telling the truth? Maybe you can't solve the crime, so you're trying to blame me!"

Ben placed the fake e-mail and a printout of the

game log-ons on the bench. "We're not making this up, Alyssa," he said calmly. "You can look at the IP addresses and time stamps yourself."

Alyssa grabbed both pages and held them in front of her face, hiding her expression from Club CSI and Whitney. When she finally lowered the pages, a triumphant smile flickered across her mouth.

"Guess what? I have an alibi," she said. "My mom. In fact, she's here in the gym right now. If you want to go talk to her, that's fine with me. In fact, I think you should."

"We already talked to your mom," Corey said. "She told us you like to use the library computers after school while she finishes her work."

"Exactly. And my mom gets off work at five!" Alyssa announced. "So by 5:09, when somebody hacked the You Can Draw It! account, we were already on our way home!"

Club CSI exchanged a glance. That was *not* what they had expected to hear.

"I mean it," Alyssa said. "Please—come talk to my mom. She's out the door at five o'clock exactly, so she can get dinner ready by the time my brothers get home. I actually remember that day. . . . She was bugging me to get *off* the computer because she wanted to leave already."

Corey observed Alyssa closely while she spoke. She didn't fidget, stammer, or show any signs that she was lying—not once.

"I believe you," Corey said.

Hannah and Ben quickly nodded.

"But you've got to help us, Alyssa," Corey continued. "You were probably at the library at the same time as the thief. Did you see anyone hanging around? Was there anybody waiting for a computer?"

"That is *soooo* freaky," Whitney said with a shiver. "Whoever stole those upgrades on my parents' credit card might have been right next to you!"

"I don't know," Alyssa said. "I honestly can't remember. I was too busy writing that stupid e-mail. I wish I'd never even sent it."

Suddenly, Corey's eyes went wide. "Did you log out?" he asked urgently. "After you sent that e-mail from Whitney's account? Did you log out?"

Alyssa paused to think about it. "No, but I didn't have to," she said. "I just closed the Internet window, and that logs you out of your e-mail."

Everyone stared at Alyssa blankly.

"You know," she tried to explain. "It's part of e-mail. When you close the Internet, the system automatically logs you out."

"Mine doesn't work that way," Hannah said. "Whenever I open a new Internet window, I'm still logged in. What e-mail program do you use?"

"We-Mail," Alyssa answered.

"But my e-mail is through SmartMail," Whitney said. "You *have* to manually log off."

"Oh," Alyssa said in a quiet voice. "I didn't know that."

"So Whitney's account was still active after Alyssa left the library," Ben concluded. "Whoever used that computer next—Dancer99, if we're right—would have opened the Internet and found Whitney's e-mail just sitting there. And she could have read all of Whitney's old e-mails."

"And I had that one!" Whitney exclaimed. "The one that You Can Draw It! sent me after I registered! It had my username *and* my password in it!"

"That's it!" Corey exclaimed. "That's how the thief got access to your account!"

"So we've figured out the *how*," Ben said. "And we already know the *why*—the prize money. But we still need to figure out the *who*. Who is Dancer99?"

Everyone was quiet for a long moment. Then Alyssa spoke. "Did you check the sign-in books?"

"Which sign-in books?" Ben asked.

"At the library, you have to sign in before you can use the computers," she explained. "No exceptions—even I have to sign in. So whoever used the computer right after me must've signed in too."

Ben started to laugh. "I can't believe it," he said to Corey and Hannah. "There was a sign-in book right there this whole time!"

"If only we'd tried to use one of the computers when we were investigating the e-mail," Hannah said. "Mrs. Gomez would've asked us to sign in, and then we would've known about it."

Corey hopped off the bleacher. "We shouldn't waste another minute. Come on—let's go to the library!"

Chapter 14

I t's over there," Alyssa whispered as she pointed toward the back of the reference librarian's desk. "That big navy blue binder."

Club CSI, Alyssa, and Whitney were camped out on the floor in the library. Corey had found the perfect aisle for conducting their investigation—nestled away in the Property Records section; it didn't get much traffic, but gave them a clear view of the reference desk . . . and the computer bank. With books and papers spread around them, they looked like any group of students working on a school project. No one would've suspected they were actually in the middle of solving a crime. They watched the reference desk for a few minutes as people walked over to the binder, signed in or out, and then walked away.

"We're going to need a few minutes with the sign-in book," Ben said, a worried frown on his face. "But Miss Wilson is right there. Won't it seem weird to a librarian if we're examining every page of the book?"

"Maybe," said Alyssa. "And Miss Wilson is pretty strict. She sees everything!"

"I have an idea," Corey said. "What if I tell her I need help finding a book? Like, I have a big project for school and I don't know where to begin?" He made a funny face. "That's actually not a lie. I really do need to start working on my social studies project this weekend."

"Sounds good," Alyssa said. "That should get Miss Wilson away from the desk long enough for me to grab the book and bring it back to you guys. Then I can hang out near the reference desk in case Miss Wilson comes back too soon, and I can distract her again."

"You don't have to do that," Hannah spoke up.

"It's no problem," Alyssa said with a shrug. "I'm here so much that no one will even notice me at the reference desk."

"Wish me luck," Corey said as he stood up.

Everyone watched as Corey chatted with Miss Wilson. Then he followed her to the back of the library, flashing a quick thumbs-up at Club CSI, Whitney, and Alyssa as he passed.

"You're up," Ben whispered to Alyssa. "Go get it!"

Alyssa casually walked toward the reference desk. She grabbed the computer sign-in book off the desk and, glancing over her shoulder for Miss Wilson, hurried back to Ben, Hannah, and Whitney.

"Here you go," she said in a hushed voice. "I'll be waiting at the desk."

Then she disappeared down the aisle.

Hannah started flipping through the book as fast as she could. "March twenty-second, March twenty-sixth, March twenty-ninth, April first, April fourth—Here it is!" she said. Hannah's finger traced down the long list of names. "Okay, Alyssa Gomez . . . signed in at 4:12, signed out at 5:01."

"So who signed in after her?" Whitney demanded.

Hannah squinted at the page. Then she frowned and shook her head. "I'm not sure," she admitted. "It's just a big, messy scrawl. I think the initials are . . . J . . . G? Maybe?"

"Wait a second," Ben said, grabbing the book

and pulling it onto his lap. "That could be an *O*, right? A fancy, frilly, weird-looking *O*?"

Hannah took another look. "Yeah," she said. "Yeah, I think it could be."

"*J. O.*," Ben said. "*J. O.* . . . jojo2020!"

"One of Dancer99's other usernames!" Hannah added.

"Quick," Ben said. "What are the other hacking dates? Let's see if J. O. signed in on the other days, too."

"Okay," Hannah said. "The next time was April sixth."

Ben scanned the page. "No J. O.," he reported, with a hint of disappointment in his voice. "But someone signed in with really loopy handwriting at 6:42."

"That's right when the hacking happened!" Hannah said excitedly. "I mean, 6:46 to be precise— but close enough."

"Maybe J. O. used a fake name every time she signed in," Ben suggested. "She thought that would keep people from connecting her with the hacking."

"You guys," Whitney said. "Alyssa's looking kind

of nervous over there. I think you'd better get the book back before Miss Wilson returns."

"We don't have enough time to look up all the hacking dates, find the fake names, and compare the handwriting to be sure," Ben said.

"I know!" Hannah said. "Let's photocopy the pages from the days when Whitney's account was hacked. Then we can take all the time we need to analyze the handwriting."

"Here," Whitney urged. "Use my copy card!"

With the sign-in book under her arm and Whitney's copy card in her hand, Hannah sprinted toward the photocopy room. A few minutes later, she emerged from the room with a triumphant smile on her face. Hannah swung by the reference desk and handed the binder to Alyssa. They put it back on the desk and opened it to that day's date. It was like it had never been taken. Then both girls joined Whitney and Ben.

"Mission accomplished!" Hannah said proudly as she placed the still-warm photocopies on the floor. Then she pressed her hand across her chest. "It's silly, but my heart is totally pounding! I got so freaked out that Miss Wilson would suddenly walk into the copy room and want to know what I was doing with the sign-in book!"

"Where's your faith?" Corey teased Hannah as he returned to the group, carrying a stack of heavy books. "I would never let you down!"

"I know that," Hannah replied with a grin.

Ben handed Whitney the list of dates when her account was hacked. "Can you read us the dates and times from this list?" he asked. "Then we'll search each page for the hacker's messy handwriting."

"Sure," Whitney said. "The next one was . . . April seventh."

"My mom worked that day," Alyssa said suddenly. "I remember because it was a Saturday and she usually doesn't work on Saturdays. She was filling in for Miss Wilson."

Then Alyssa gasped and clutched Whitney's arm. "I was *right here* at the same time that Whitney's account was being hacked!"

"That is all so freaky," Whitney whispered.

The group worked quietly for several minutes, identifying ten different signatures that corresponded with the hackings.

"All right," Corey said as he lined up each photocopy so that the suspicious signatures were arranged in a neat row. "Let's start analyzing."

"Even if we weren't looking at photocopies, we wouldn't have to worry about the kind of paper or the type of pen that was used," Ben began. "Every page of the sign-in book is the same, and it looks like everyone signed with a ballpoint pen."

Alyssa nodded. "Yeah, there's a blue one on a chain right next to the sign-in book," she confirmed.

"So our main focus will be the handwriting itself," Ben continued. He leaned down to get a closer look. "Check out all the loops and swirls. It's really artistic looking, isn't it?"

"That's what makes it so hard to read—some of the letters are overlapping," Hannah said. She pointed at the upper case _O_ in the first signature. "That's why I thought the _O_ was a _G_ when I first saw it."

"And each one of these signatures slants far to the right," Corey observed. "But the biggest thing I noticed is the way the _I_s are dotted. See that? Every single _I_ has a big, open circle over it. It's really distinctive."

"So I think it's pretty obvious that all these signatures are from the same person—even though she used different names," Hannah said. "But this is kind of weird. I think I found an additional signature from last night—April twenty-seventh."

She handed the photocopy around so that everyone could see it.

"J. O.," Corey said. He frowned. "It's identical to the signature from the first hacking on April fourth. But why would the hacker suddenly start using her real name again?"

Everyone thought about Corey's question. Then Ben's eyes lit up. "Look at the date!" he exclaimed. "That's the day *after* we sent messages to Dancer99, jojo2020, and LOL1234 . . . and two days after we investigated at Whitney's house!"

"Which means it was two days after my parents unlinked the credit card, too," Whitney realized.

"Dancer99 realized her expansion-pack spree was over," Ben deduced, "so when she stopped hacking, she also stopped signing in with fake names."

"Then her real initials *are* J. O.," said Corey.

"It means something else, too," Hannah said. "It means she's still coming to the library to use the computers—and she's signing in with her real name again!"

"We're going to catch her," Corey said eagerly. "I just know it. We'll have to take shifts hanging out here and monitoring the sign-in book—"

"But we have to be careful," Ben interrupted, shaking his head. "J. O. is here a *lot*. If we're suddenly staring at the sign-in book every day, she might get suspicious."

"I know," Alyssa spoke up. "I can do it. I'm already here every afternoon, so it won't be weird at all for me to hang out near the reference desk. Sometimes I help my mom with filing and stuff, anyway."

"So you can keep a close eye on the sign-in book, and the *minute* you see J. O.'s signature, text us," Hannah told her. "We'll come right over."

"And make sure you don't, like, try to talk to her or anything without us," Ben added.

"Thanks, Alyssa," Corey said. "This is the biggest break in the case we've had so far. If you hadn't told us about the sign-in sheets, we'd still be at a total dead end."

"No problem," Alyssa replied. "I'm just glad you still don't think I did it."

Hannah turned to Ben and Corey. "I'm thinking

it's time we told Officer Inverno about the case," she said. "Especially if we might meet up with J. O. soon."

"For real? You're going to the *police*?" Whitney asked, her eyes wide. "That seems so serious."

"Yeah. But what happened to you was a crime," Ben explained. "And Officer Inverno likes to know what we're up to . . . especially when we're going to confront a suspect."

Corey started stacking up his pile of books.

"Oh, I can put those books back on the shelves, Corey," Alyssa said as she reached for the pile.

"Put them back?" Corey asked. He shook his head. "No, I need to check them out. I really do have to start working on my project!"

When Club CSI stopped by the police station, they found Officer Inverno sitting at his desk. "It's Woodlands's best junior detectives!" he said as he ushered them into his office. "What can I do for you?"

"Sorry to bother you, Officer Inverno," Hannah began. "I hope we're not interrupting anything important."

"I'm just catching up on some paperwork," Officer Inverno replied, gesturing to the stack of folders before him. "The job isn't all excitement and adventure—but you've probably realized that already!"

"We've been working on a new case," Ben said. "And I think we're getting close to solving it."

Officer Inverno leaned back in his chair with an interested look on his face. "Tell me everything," he said.

Ever since Club CSI's very first case, Officer Inverno had supported them in any way that he could—while always looking out for their safety. As Ben, Corey, and Hannah told him the facts of their current case, Officer Inverno started taking notes in a small notebook. He stopped to ask a few questions as they presented the evidence: the dates and times of when Whitney's You Can Draw It! account was hacked; the stolen expansion packs that were gifted to Dancer99, jojo2020, and LOL1234; the printout of IP addresses and the map that led them to the library; and, finally, the photocopies of the sign-in sheets. Officer Inverno examined each piece of evidence carefully without saying a word. When he finally looked up, there was a smile on his face.

"Excellent investigative work, Club CSI," he said. "You've done a great job here—and I agree that you're close to solving this one."

Hannah, Corey, and Ben grinned at one another.

"But I have one request for you," Officer Inverno continued. "When you get word that your suspect is at the library, I want you to call me right away. I don't *think* Dancer99 is dangerous, but I want to be on the scene when you confront him or her."

"We will," Hannah said at once. "Promise."

Officer Inverno rose as Ben, Hannah, and Corey packed up the evidence they had collected. "Good luck," he said. "I expect I'll be seeing you soon."

Chapter 15

O fficer Inverno was right: Alyssa's text to Club CSI came just three days later.

    J. O. IS HERE!!!! signed
    in 5 min ago. sitting @
    computer 3 right now!!!

Luckily, the members of Club CSI were close to the library. Ben responded immediately.

    on our way!

The bus ride to the library only took ten minutes, but it felt like an eternity to Corey. "What if she leaves before we get there?" he asked, drumming his fingers anxiously. "Man, is this bus taking the scenic route or what?"

"Relax," Hannah told him. "J. O. just logged in for some computer time. I bet she'll be there for a while."

Ben stared at a floorplan of the library on his Quark Pad. "This time, we should go straight to the Pottery and Ceramics section," he said. "It's not as exciting as the Science section, but I think if we slip a couple books off the shelf, we'll have a perfect view of Computer Three."

The bus's brakes screeched as it stopped in front of the library. Corey leaped into the aisle. "Let's do this!" he exclaimed.

Inside the library, Club CSI crept down the aisles in total silence, trying to act as casually as they could. They could see Alyssa leaning against the reference desk, chatting quietly with her mom—but her eyes never left the computer bank.

In the Ceramics aisle, Hannah slid three books off the shelf, making a small window that was just the right size for the friends to finally get a glimpse of the hacker. When she realized who it was, Hannah was so shocked that her hands flew up to her face. She immediately covered her mouth so that her gasp of surprise wouldn't attract attention.

"I can't believe it!" she whispered to Ben and Corey. "I mean, I never, never, *never* would have guessed . . ."

"Me neither," Corey whispered back. He didn't look away from the suspect for even a second. "Wait, what's her name again?"

"Jessica," Hannah whispered. "Jessica Olivera. We've been taking dance classes at Pirouette together for five years. She's always been so friendly. Even though she's in high school, she never acts like she's cooler or better than everybody else. She helps *everybody* learn the toughest steps! I just—I never would've guessed . . ." Hannah's voice trailed off for a moment as she thought about it. "Then again, a bunch of things *do* make sense. I mean, Jessica loves to dance, so the Dancer99 username fits—and so does jojo2020, with her initials. And she only played in the evenings—after Pirouette closes. And you guys saw that mural. She's really artistic. No wonder Jessica is obsessed with You Can Draw It!"

"Obsessed enough to steal, though?" Corey asked.

"I don't know," Hannah admitted. "I guess—I guess it's not official until we see Jessica logged in as Dancer99."

Ben squinted as he tried to get a closer look at Computer Three's screen. "I just can't tell from here," he said in frustration. "We're going to have to get closer . . . maybe talk to Jessica . . ."

"Then we have to call Officer Inverno," Hannah said, reaching for her phone.

Corey shook his head. "We can't call him unless we're sure . . . *really* sure," he said. "I mean, what if we're wrong? If we start wasting his time, Officer Inverno won't take us seriously anymore."

"But I promised," Hannah argued.

"I think Corey's right," Ben said with a frown. "What if one of us walks past Jessica and just talks to her a little? Just to find out her username, if we can—*not* to confront her or anything. And if she really *is* Dancer99, we'll call Officer Inverno before we actually confront her." He turned to Hannah. "You know her best. Want to give it a try?"

Hannah looked worried. "I don't know if I can," she said frankly. "Jessica and I might know each other *too* well. If she can tell I'm nervous—"

"I'll go," Corey volunteered. "It won't be totally weird for me to talk to her, since you introduced us a few weeks ago."

"You'll do great, Corey," Hannah whispered, giving his arm a quick squeeze. "Just get her username. That's all you have to do."

"Oh no!" Ben suddenly exclaimed.

"What? What happened?" Corey and Hannah asked at the same time.

"Whitney's here!" Ben replied, pointing at the glass door to the library. "And she looks ready for a fight!"

Chapter 16

"Oh no. No, no, no, no," Corey said. "Alyssa must have texted her, too! If Jessica sees Whitney, she will split for sure. She knows it was Whitney's e-mail account and Whitney's You Can Draw It! account! We've gotta—"

"On it," Hannah replied. She darted to the door just as Whitney stepped inside. Ben and Corey followed Hannah as she pulled Whitney into an aisle.

"Please, Whitney, you've got to wait outside until we figure out if Dancer99 is Jessica's username," Hannah said.

"No way! I'm sick of waiting!" Whitney argued. "I can't believe *Jessica* hacked my account, stole my parents' money, got me grounded, and almost ruined my party! She's *not* getting away with it!"

"Exactly—we've almost caught her," Ben said urgently. "But if she sees you and takes off before we can confirm that she's Dancer99, she might actually get away with it."

"Officer Inverno promised he'd come as soon as we know Dancer99's real identity," added Corey. "You just have to be patient for a few more minutes."

Whitney's eyes flashed angrily, but she had to admit Club CSI was right. "So what do you want me to do?" she asked.

"Wait outside to make sure Jessica doesn't see you," Ben told her. "If Jessica really is Dancer99, you'll have a chance to tell her how you feel about what she did."

Whitney nodded without saying a word. Then she turned around and left the library.

"Corey, go," Ben said. "I don't know how much time we have before Jessica leaves!"

Corey was already on his way to the computer bank. As he walked, he psyched himself up for the most important moment of the entire investigation.

"Jessica?" he said as he passed behind Computer Three. "Is that you? Hey, it's me, Corey—Hannah's friend."

It took a second for Jessica to place Corey, but as soon as she recognized him, a big smile spread across her face. "Hey, Corey, what's up?" she asked.

"Just getting some homework done," he replied. "What are you up to? A little You Can Draw It!, huh? I love that game."

"Oh, this is just a picture I've been working on," she replied, nodding her head at the computer screen. "I'm having some trouble with the beams of sunlight shining on the snowy mountains. I don't know, what do you think? It looks kind of fake to me."

"Fake?" Corey repeated, shaking his head. "No way. That drawing is awesome! I can't believe you made it! Man, Hannah said you were crazy talented, but now I see for myself it's true."

Jessica's smile grew even bigger. "Really? You think so?" she asked.

"For sure," Corey replied. "I bet you could win that big contest they're having."

"Oh, I hope so!" Jessica exclaimed. "I have to enter my drawing by midnight—that's the deadline. Could I ask you a big favor? If I make it into the top twenty-five . . . would you vote for me?"

Corey's heart started pounding. This was it—the big moment.

"Sure," he said. "What's your username?"

"It's Dancer99," Jessica replied as her eyes drifted back to the screen. She frowned a little, then switched over to an expansion pack that offered different sparkle effects. With a click of her mouse, Jessica's snowy mountain started to gleam. "There. That's better, isn't it?"

"Yeah," Corey said. He swallowed hard. "Um, see you around, Jessica."

"Bye, Corey," Jessica replied, adjusting the color on her picture. She looked up to give him another smile. "Thanks again for voting for me!"

Corey felt funny as he walked back to Hannah and Ben. Hannah was right about Jessica; she was incredibly nice. It was hard to believe that she was the same person who had stolen all those expansion packs by hacking into Whitney's account.

But it didn't matter how nice Jessica seemed. What she had done was wrong—really wrong. And it was time for her to be held responsible.

"Call Officer Inverno," he said in a strained whisper. "It's her. Dancer99."

Chapter 17

Club CSI moved fast. While Ben went outside to call Officer Inverno, Hannah slipped away to tell Alyssa and Mrs. Gomez what they had discovered. Corey, meanwhile, kept an eye on Jessica to make sure she didn't leave before Officer Inverno arrived.

Then everything seemed to happen at once: Officer Inverno, Ben, and Whitney walked into the library just as Hannah waved to Corey from an empty meeting room where they could confront Jessica.

"Jessica?" Corey said.

She spun around in her chair. This time her smile wasn't quite so big. "Hey, Corey, do you need something else?" Jessica asked.

"Actually," Corey replied. "I need to talk to you."

Corey made a motion for Jessica to follow him, but she only turned back to the computer. "I'm really busy with this drawing. Like I said earlier, the deadline's tonight."

"We can do this here, but I doubt you'd want to," warned Corey.

Jessica looked up at Corey again, and this time she had suspicion in her eyes.

"Um, I think I'm going to go," said Jessica. "I can finish this drawing somewhere else. You're starting to weird me out."

Jessica grabbed her bag, jumped up from her chair, and moved toward the front door . . . only to run smack into Officer Inverno, who had been standing off to the side.

"Hello, young lady," Officer Inverno said. "Would you please come with me?"

All the color drained from Jessica's face, leaving her pale and ashen. "What do you—I don't—What?" she stammered.

"Come," Corey said. "Let's go somewhere quiet."

Jessica looked like she might want to make a run for it, but then she sighed. She nodded and turned the other way.

"Oh, you'll want to log out of your game," Ben spoke up. "Leaving your account open on a public computer is a bad idea. A *really* bad idea. You never know who might steal your information."

Jessica went over to Computer Three and clicked the mouse a couple times, still moving in a daze. Then she followed Corey over to the conference room where Hannah, Alyssa, and Mrs. Gomez were waiting. The small room was pretty crowded when Corey, Ben, Officer Inverno, Jessica, and Whitney joined them, but there were enough chairs for everyone.

"Have a seat, Miss Olivera," Officer Inverno said. Then he glanced over toward Corey, Ben, and Hannah. "Club CSI, go ahead."

"Jessica, is Dancer99 your You Can Draw It! username?" Ben began.

Jessica started to shake her head—but a piercing look from Corey reminded her that she had already told him it was.

Jessica swallowed a few times, as if her mouth was suddenly dry, and bit her lower lip. "Um, yeah. So what?" she asked, glancing at the door. She seemed like she wanted to run out of that little room more than anything in the world.

"Well, we have reason to believe that the person behind Dancer99 stole ten expansion packs by hacking into another person's You Can Draw It! account," Ben continued.

"N-no way," Jessica said. "I didn't do—what, *hacking*? I don't know, like, anything about computers."

But as she said that, Jessica began wringing her hands together. She bit her lip and pressed them together, like she didn't want to say another word.

"So those expansion packs you were just using," Corey said. "How did you get them?"

"Um . . . I b-bought them. Of course. Like everybody does," she said.

"Can you prove that?" Hannah asked. "Because we think that those packs were purchased through Whitney's account, gifted to several other accounts, then transferred to Dancer99."

"Well, maybe . . . maybe . . . maybe *my* account was hacked too!" Jessica blurted out. "Maybe your 'hacker' is transferring stolen expansion packs through my account! Did you think of that, maybe?"

Club CSI exchanged a troubled glance. It was so clear to them that Jessica was lying, and yet they had never expected her to deny the charges like this.

"Okay. Let's explore that possibility," Ben said. "When you noticed ten new expansion packs in your account, did you contact Customer Service? Did you tell anyone your account had been hacked? Or did you just start using the expansion packs? Like you had every right to them?"

"I—I—I thought they were, like, free upgrades or something," Jessica said.

"Wait, I'm confused." Corey frowned. "First you said you bought the expansion packs. Now you are saying that maybe your account was hacked and that you thought the expansion packs were free upgrades? Which one is it, Jessica?"

Jessica's eyes darted back and forth nervously. "I don't know!" she replied.

"Well, *I* know! You stole them—using *my* account!" Whitney yelled so loudly that everyone in the conference room jumped.

"Whitney. I know you're upset. But this is still a library," Mrs. Gomez interrupted her. "Shhh!"

Everyone chuckled a little—except for Whitney and Jessica. When Whitney spoke again, her lowered voice was worse than her yelling.

"These guys have *evidence*," Whitney hissed.

"And they can show it to you, and you can come up with a bunch of different lies, but that doesn't change the truth. You got *my* password, you logged on to *my* account, you bought expansion packs with *my* parents' credit card, and *I* got grounded for it! There's only one word for what you did: stealing. And that makes you a thief!"

Officer Inverno cleared his throat like he was about to intervene. But before he could, Jessica buried her face in her hands. Then she started to cry. No one spoke. When Jessica finally looked up, her face was blotchy and streaked with tears.

"I know that," Jessica said. She shuddered a little as she wiped her eyes. Everyone waited while Jessica took a deep breath and tried to calm down.

"I mean, it didn't feel like stealing when I did it." Jessica's voice was halting as she struggled to find the right words. "I just clicked the mouse, you know? I know this sounds stupid, but I just didn't think about the fact that it was someone else's account—and someone else's money. I am *so* sorry. I will pay you back every penny, I promise."

"Jessica, you should know I'll be contacting the people at You Can Draw It!" Officer Inverno spoke up. "I expect they'll close your account and report you to the credit card company for fraud."

"And I'm going to need your library card," Mrs. Gomez added. "Your library privileges are suspended for illegal activity and misuse of library computers."

Jessica nodded silently as she slid her card across the table to Mrs. Gomez. It seemed like there wasn't much more to say. But Corey had one more question for the girl who was Dancer99.

"Why did you do it?" he asked.

"For the contest," Jessica said simply. "I wanted to go to dance camp so badly this summer. If I'd won the grand prize, I could. But there's no way you can win unless you have a bunch of upgrades. It's not *fair*. Everyone should have all the same tools, not just the people who can buy expansion packs!"

Jessica took another deep breath. "But that doesn't matter," she continued in a quieter voice. "There's no excuse for what I did. I'm—I'm truly sorry, Whitney, and I hope you can forgive me."

Whitney had her arms crossed, but her angry expression softened a little. "I'll try," Whitney replied honestly.

Chapter 18

The sun was just starting to set on Friday night when Hannah reached for the doorbell. Then she paused and turned to Corey and Ben. "Ready?" she asked.

"As ready as I'll ever be," Ben replied. He sounded a little nervous. "What if we're the only seventh graders here?"

"Oh relax," Corey said confidently. "It's a party! It'll be fun! And besides, they're just eighth graders. They don't bite!" Then Corey's smile faded. "Well, I guess vampire eighth graders do. But we don't have to worry about that . . . right?"

Before Hannah could answer Corey, or even ring the doorbell, the door swung open. Alyssa must have been watching for them. "I thought you guys would never get here!" she exclaimed, but Club CSI could tell from her smile that Alyssa wasn't mad. She led them downstairs to the basement, where strands of tiny lights twinkled across the ceiling. Whitney's laptop was hooked up to the speakers, playing a nonstop stream of dance music so loud that Corey could feel it pulsing in his chest.

"Party can start now, everybody!" Alyssa shouted.

"Awesome!" cheered Whitney.

Then, to Club CSI's surprise, a group of eighth graders swarmed, asking lots of questions.

"How did you figure out that the hacker was using the library computers?"

"What made you think all three usernames were for the same person?"

"Where did you learn all that computer investigation stuff? You guys are awesome!"

"Enough!" Whitney said, laughing as she pushed through the crowd. "Let them get some pizza or brownies or something first. Then you can ask them whatever you want." She pulled Club CSI over to a table that was crowded with food. "Sorry about that. *Everyone* has been wanting to meet you!"

"Really?" asked Ben.

"Oh yeah. You guys are practically the guests of honor. We all know that my party would've been canceled if you didn't prove to my parents I was innocent," Whitney replied. "I swear, it's like the whole school has been talking about it all week!"

"Yeah, we kind of figured that when Miss Hodges heard about Jessica getting busted before we even had a chance to tell her!" Corey replied.

Ben and Hannah looked at each other. It was obvious they were both thinking about the part that Corey had left out. Miss Hodges had been impressed by their investigation, as always, and she had praised them for the way they'd managed to solve such a tricky case. But she had also warned Club CSI that their investigations might get a little more complicated as their reputation spread . . . and potential suspects tried to avoid them.

Corey wasn't too worried, though. It seemed clear to him that Club CSI's knowledge and techniques improved with each investigation. At least, that's what had happened with his interview skills.

So Corey had a feeling that no matter what happened next, Club CSI would be ready to tackle the case!

Ellie O'Ryan doodles on just about every scrap of paper within arm's reach, but she's never gotten in trouble for it . . . yet! Ellie has written more than two hundred books for children and young adults, and has loved reading, writing, and solving mysteries since she was a kid herself. She lives with her family in North Carolina.